CATHY'S CHRISTMAS CONFESSION

A CHRISTMAS RIDGE ROMANCE
BOOK THREE

PATTI SHENE GONZALES

STEP INTO THE LIGHT MEDIA

CATHY'S CHRISTMAS CONFESSION: A CHRISTMAS RIDGE ROMANCE, BOOK 3

Published by Step Into the Light Media
Las Aninas, CO

Copyright © 2023 by Patti Shene Gonzales
All rights reserved.

No part of this book may be reproduced, or stored in a retrieval system, or transmitted in any form by or by any means, electronic, mechanical, photocopying, recording, or otherwise, without express written permission of the publisher.

ISBN: 979-8-9879611-0-0

Cover design by: Virginia McKevitt

The characters and events portrayed in this book or fictitious. Any similarity to real persons, living or dead, is coincidental, and not intended by the author.

All Scripture quotations, unless otherwise indicated, are taken from the Holy Bible, New International Version®, NIV®. Copyright ©1973, 1978, 1984, 2011 by Biblica, Inc.™ Used by permission of Zondervan. All rights reserved worldwide. www.zondervan.com

All rights reserved by Patti Sheen Gonzales and Step Into the Light Media.

To all those with a hole in their heart
May you find Christmas joy
Happy Jesus's birthday

Gwen -

May you always

find christmas joy!

Patti Sherri Gonzales

CHAPTER 1

Cathy Fischer chiseled at the thick ice encasing the windshield of her gunmetal gray Dodge Ram. Snow blew in her face, slithered down her neck, and crunched under her feet.

Why spend time today on what could be put off until tomorrow? Or the next day. Six decades of this philosophy that had caused her grief more than once was playing havoc again.

Ice wouldn't have formed under a foot of snow blanketing her truck if a dead garage door battery hadn't prevented her from putting the vehicle in the garage. That's where it belonged during an overnight Colorado winter storm. She'd intended to replace the battery days ago.

By the time she cleared the windows, the defroster had left a peep hole in the windshield.

Snow covered the roof. Should she stand on the running board and clear it?

Nah.

That frozen icing would stay right where it was on this metal cupcake.

She backed down the driveway and waited as a black SUV crept up the road. The white stuff fell in a heavy curtain, reducing visibility to less than a quarter of a mile. Wind whipped the shards of icy precipitation against her windshield. She kept a safe distance from the vehicle ahead and tested her brake.

Just in case.

Sure enough.

Slick pavement.

Should she have opted for safety and stayed home? Pastor Hewitt would have understood if she'd called and told him she wouldn't be in today due to the weather. That would only make it tough on her. Deadlines needed to be met by the end of the year and time was running out. Her write-in desk calendar would soon display the month of December. Living a few miles out of town had its disadvantages, but she seldom let inclement weather stop her from going anywhere she needed to go.

Cathy concentrated on the snow-packed road, trying not to drift over the center line or too close to the embankment on the right.

Her neck muscles tightened.

The closer she came to town, the more the snow tapered off. Visibility improved and a patch of blue sky appeared. Sunshine filtered through the clouds and bathed the new fallen snow in millions of tiny sparkling pinpoints of light.

She relaxed and reached for her travel mug of hot coffee.

It wasn't there.

Drat!

Of course not. It was sitting in the snow where she'd left it when clearing the truck.

CATHY'S CHRISTMAS CONFESSION

Her spirits plummeted. She'd managed to concoct the brew just right this morning, not like other days when she ended up with either colored water on her tongue or coffee grounds in her teeth.

She sulked over the absence of her favorite drink. Why couldn't she ever remember what she—

A stop sign loomed ahead. How had it come up so quickly?

She tapped the brake.

The sign drew closer.

She pressed harder.

Too hard.

A barrage of snow cascaded off the roof, slid down the windshield, and obscured her view.

The pickup spun in a three hundred sixty degree turn like a top in the hands of a toddler. All sense of orientation fled. Metal screeched against metal on the passenger side. Her body lurched forward, then slammed against the back of the driver's seat, restricted by her seat belt.

Dear God, no!

She'd hit something.

Her heart bounded in her chest. Had she hurt someone? Killed them perhaps? Her hands shook. She couldn't control them enough to unfasten her seat belt.

Calm down. A church bell chimed.

The airbag hadn't deployed, so the damage couldn't be that bad.

Could it?

Her hands steadier now, Cathy released the seat belt. She tightened her scarf around her neck and eased open the door. Fluffy snow engulfed her feet and filtered inside her boots as she stepped down.

3

Silence enveloped her. Even the church bell had ceased its calming tones.

The truck's front wheels were embedded in a bank of snow and mud thrown up from the street by a snowplow. The stop sign towered above her. She glared at it as though it had jumped out and smacked her. Thank goodness the thing was encased in cement, preventing it from toppling into her vehicle.

Her heartrate returned to normal.

She peered at her image in the sideview mirror. No blood in sight.

Good.

She had escaped injury to herself or anyone else. Even the sign appeared intact. Should she report the accident? Probably.

Cathy climbed back into the vehicle and searched for her cell phone. She hardly ever used the gadget, but she had the local sheriff on speed dial. She heard a soft knock on her window and cracked it open.

A man dressed in a blue jacket with deep set blue eyes and a full head of gray hair waved a greeting. "Cathy, I thought that was your vehicle. Are you okay?"

David Martin. She'd not seen him for a while, but she'd recognize his resonant voice anywhere. "I'm fine. Thanks for stopping. I was looking for my cell phone so I can call the cops."

"I wouldn't bother to report it. Why don't we just try to see if we can get you out of here?"

"Well, all right. I do have kitty litter in the back. That should help."

"And I have a shovel if we need it."

She got out of the car and they slogged through thick, wet

snow to the rear of the truck. "Are you sure I shouldn't report this?"

"Who's going to know?" He looked up and down the street. "I don't see anybody else around."

"God would know. After all, I am the church secretary now." She furrowed her brow. "Have to keep up a certain image."

"God has common sense. He'd probably tell you not to report it either."

DAVID GROANED AS RED AND BLUE FLASHES OF LIGHT cascaded across the snow. A police cruiser inched up behind the truck. He leaned in close to Cathy as he reached for the kitty litter. "Guess you don't have a choice now. Play innocent. Don't tell him you weren't going to—"

He jumped back as a police officer approached, clipboard in hand. Ear muffs peeked out from under his uniform hat and a stern expression clouded his face.

"I'm officer Greenwald." He stood between Cathy and David. "Who's responsible for this accident?"

Cathy faced him with a wary grin. "That's my truck."

"Are you injured?"

"Just my pride."

No response to her attempt at humor. "May I see your license—"

His words were interrupted by a high-pitched screech from the house across the street. "She did it, Mr. Policeman. I saw the whole thing. She's a terrible driver. Take her license away."

All three turned their attention to the distraught woman.

Nellie Crabtree's head, crowned with thin gray tufts of hair, jutted out from an upstairs window.

David grinned and Cathy chuckled, but the officer's face remained impassive. He strode out into the center of the street, closer to Nellie's yard. "I'm handling the situation, ma'am. Better get your head inside where it's warm and shut that window."

"She almost hit my Christmas tree!" She pointed toward a pine tree in her front yard with a strand of lights looped over low-hanging branches. "She's dangerous!"

"Yes, ma'am." Officer Greenwald turned back toward Cathy and David, a look of distress creasing his stern features.

The window slammed shut and the gray-haired woman disappeared from view.

"As I was saying." The policeman glanced into the truck bed as he walked past it, "I need to see your license and registration, please."

David folded his arms across his chest. "Look, Officer, I don't believe anyone can be held responsible. Seems like a simple case of poor road conditions." He chuckled. "Unless you listen to Mrs. Crabtree."

The joke fell flat. "Nothing is ever a simple case. There's always a reason, usually negligence." The officer lifted his clipboard.

David bristled at the cop's brusque manner. "Accidents do happen."

Officer Greenwald looked up and fixed David with a stony glare. "What's your name?"

"David Martin, but I—"

"Did you witness the accident, sir?"

"No. I just stopped to see if Cathy needed help."

6

He scoffed. "Then please allow the offender to provide the information I need."

Offender? You'd think she'd cleaned out a jewelry store at gunpoint.

Cathy handed over some cards. "License, registration, and proof of insurance."

"Is this your correct address?" The officer's pen scratched across paper.

"Yes. Everything is current."

"And this is your vehicle?" He glanced at the truck.

David shoved his hands in his pockets. Didn't the officer read her registration with the make, model, and license number? He bit back a comment and kept his mouth shut.

"Yes, sir." Cathy appeared unfazed.

Officer Greenwald trudged through the snow to the stop sign. Cathy fell in behind him. David tagged along, keeping his distance. The officer ran his hand along the length of the metal pole. "Significant damage here. The city may bill you for the repair."

Significant damage? How could a tiny dent constitute significant damage?

The words David had swallowed earlier poured out of his mouth in a torrent. "Can't you show a little consideration? The roads are terrible today. Anyone could have done what she did."

Officer Greenwald, much shorter than David, gave him a look that put David in the category of a worm to be squished under his boot. The policeman's cap dipped below the hood of the car, then bobbed up again. "Your headlight is broken. You'll need to get that fixed. The door is dented where you hit and there's damage to the fender." He tapped the clipboard against the door, then waved it toward the fender as though Cathy couldn't see for herself. "It's drivable, though. Wait here." He strode to his police cruiser.

He spoke into his radio, waited a moment, then stomped over and stood in front of Cathy. "Why didn't you report this?"

Cathy stammered. "I-I was looking for my cell phone when you pulled up, sir."

"That's right." David cut in. "Drivers are told not to have a cell phone within reach. It's distracting. Right?"

The officer grimaced and shook his head. "Good thing someone reported this or I'd be charging you with leaving the scene. As it is, you're getting off with careless driving and damage to public property. You need to pay the fine by the date reflected on the ticket, or you can appear in court to contest the charges. The city will notify you about a fine if it applies." The officer thrust the clipboard at Cathy. "Sign here."

David's face heated. "I'd fight this in court if I were you." The words were out of his mouth before he could stifle them. "I don't see where you're at fault here."

Cathy signed without comment and handed the clipboard back.

Officer Greenwald tore the top page off.

Cathy reached for it.

He glared at David. "I've seen enough of these accidents to know the driver didn't exercise appropriate caution for the weather conditions. She applied the brake too hard, and probably not as soon as she should have to safely complete the stop." The officer turned abruptly away.

David's gut reacted like a child chastised for asking a stupid question in class.

CATHY'S CHRISTMAS CONFESSION

"Any questions, Mrs. Fischer?" The inflection in his voice gave David a clear warning to keep quiet. He did.

"No, Officer." Cathy flashed a bright smile. "Thank you. God bless the rest of your day. Merry Christmas."

"Sure. Sure." Officer Greenwald cleared his throat and plodded through the snow back to his police cruiser.

David stared after him, then faced Cathy with a frown. "Nice guy."

She scanned the traffic ticket and shook her head. "You were very noble, but he's right. I deserved a ticket."

David clasped his gloved hands. "He was rude."

She shrugged. "He was doing his job. He called it right. I wasn't paying attention. I came up on the intersection much too fast, hit my brake too hard." She pocketed the paper. "Thank you for coming to my defense, though." She slapped him on the arm. "A few more words out of you and we both would have been hauled off to jail."

"Mrs. Crabtree almost sealed the deal. What's her problem?"

"She's wilder than a weasel around me ever since I voiced opposition to her choice of double latte brown for the church ladies' restroom walls. Accused me of stealing her cat a couple of weeks ago. I have no idea what her cat looks like. She probably doesn't even have one."

He grunted. "Sorry I lost my temper."

"You've got to give credit where it's warranted. He did say 'please.'"

CHAPTER 2

Cathy pulled into the empty church parking lot, relieved to see some kind soul had cleared enough space to allow for her vehicle and a couple of others to park. A shoveled path led along the sidewalk to the front door as well. Pastor Hewitt's vehicle wasn't in sight. Perhaps the storm had him running late. She gathered her purse, again lamenting the absence of her abandoned coffee.

She reached in the back seat and pulled out a plastic container filled with cookies. She held her breath as she opened the lid. She had forgotten all about them. Had they been damaged in the accident? From what she could see, the ones on top appeared intact. She'd inspect further when she got inside. They were probably fine since she'd wrapped them individually and separated them into plastic bags. If they had been loose in the container, she probably would have had nothing but crumbs.

The front door lock posed a problem again. She applied pressure on the key to turn the heavy tumbler. It wouldn't budge. Why did this thing work as smooth as butter one day and stick like a fly in syrup the next?

Fearful she would break the key, she attempted to withdraw it from the lock. It held fast as though a giant fist clutched it in its grasp. Great. She set her overstuffed purse on the ground next to the cookies and tugged harder. A blast of snow plopped from a tree branch and landed on top of the purse. She grabbed the satchel, brushed the snow off with her gloved hand, and leaned against the door. *Lord, a little help here please?*

Cathy took a deep breath and gave the stubborn key another yank. The metal slid easily out of the keyhole, knocking her off balance. She flailed her arms to keep from falling backward. A car horn sounded. She turned and waved, unable to identify the driver, but hoping whoever it was had not witnessed her clumsy effort to stay on her feet.

Five minutes later, after wading through a snowdrift, she gained access to the building through the side door. The lingering smell of pizza hung in the air, probably remnants of the snack the youth group had enjoyed last evening. She deposited her purse in the office and headed for the kitchen. She placed the cookies on the counter to be used by the decorating committee later in the week.

Coffee.

She seldom used the church coffeemaker, but this morning, her body begged for the brew. This contraption posed more of a challenge than her simple add-coffee-and-water-and-flip-the-switch appliance at home. Good thing someone had been considerate enough to post the instructions on the front of the machine. She followed them to the letter, not wanting to be responsible for any damage to the monstrosity.

She returned to the office to find the red light blinking on the answering machine. A message from Pastor Hewitt informed her he had opted to do hospital visits today.

The front door creaked open. Cathy stepped into the hallway. "Hey, Marge." She smiled a welcome greeting to her close friend, the church organist.

"Hi. What happened to your truck?" Worry lines furrowed Marge's brow.

"I slid into a stop sign. Got buried in a snowdrift. Got ticketed. Got yelled at by Nellie Crabtree."

"Oh, no!" Marge's hand flew to her mouth. "Anybody hurt? How much was the ticket? What was Nellie yelling about?"

"Whoa." Cathy waved her palm in a circle in front of Marge's face. "Hold on. One question at a time."

"Sorry."

"Come on. I need coffee, which caused the problem in the first place. My lack thereof, that is. I fixed some in the kitchen." She pointed to Marge's travel cup. "Do you need yours refilled?"

"No, I'm good, but I'll tag along. I want to hear this story."

Disappointment gripped Cathy as they walked down the hall. Why wasn't her sensitive nose detecting the aroma of fresh brewed coffee? She rounded the corner, stopped, and stared at the empty carafe. "What in the world?"

Marge stepped up behind her. She brushed past Cathy to the coffee machine, picked up the cord, and twirled it between her fingers. "Works better when you plug it in."

Cathy groaned. "I should have known when I was in the office and didn't smell coffee that something was wrong."

13

"Easily remedied." Marge connected the plug into the wall socket.

"Cookies! Yours?" Marge eyed the treats with a greedy glint in her eye. She opened the container top.

"Hands off." Cathy came over and swatted Marge's hands. "They're for the decorating committee."

"I'm on the decorating committee." Marge pushed out her lip in a pout.

"Yes, I know, but we don't decorate until Thursday night."

"Why'd you bring them so early? You know what a temptation they are." She gave Cathy a fiendish grin.

Cathy pointed her thumb at herself. "Because I know me. I'm so forgetful that I'd walk out the door without them, so I brought them ahead of time."

"Good thinking." Marge peered inside the container again. "Oh, snickerdoodles, my favorite. And the chocolate surprise ones. Yum!"

"Better check them and be sure none of them got broken in the accident."

"Oh, yeah, tell me what happened." Marge pulled out the plastic bags and inspected the cookies.

"It all started when I left my coffee in the snow where I set it down to clean off the truck, which I wouldn't have had to do if the truck was in the garage where it belongs, but I couldn't put it there because…"

She related the story from the accident through the police officer's ticket, David Martin stopping to help, and Nellie's outburst.

After Cathy poured a cup of liquid caffeine, the two women moved to the office, each with a cookie in hand. "David didn't like that the police officer gave me a ticket. Put up quite a squawk about it, although it wasn't any of his affair." She sighed. "It was my fault."

"Why? The roads are treacherous."

"Suppose I had run into an oncoming vehicle, killed someone? Would it still not be my fault?"

"Okay, I see your point, sort of. Still, it was only a stop sign. What set Nellie off?"

Cathy waved a hand. "I don't know. She wanted my license taken away, accused me of trying to hit her Christmas tree."

Marge chuckled. "She's a piece of work all right."

"It's not all her fault. She's got mental illness problems. I heard she spent a couple of years in the state hospital in Pueblo. Poor old soul probably doesn't have anyone to look after her."

Marge pulled a nail file from her purse and waved it in the air. "So, who's all planning to help decorate Thursday evening?"

"Pastor Hewitt and I. You. Probably a few of the youth group teens will show up. Maybe a couple of parents with the younger kids." Cathy finished her cookie and took a swig of coffee.

"Any idea who we can get to hang the greens this year? Tom Prescott can't climb a ladder with his broken foot." Cathy jotted a note on her calendar to give him a call to see how he was getting along.

"Maybe one of the youth group kids."

"I don't think Pastor Hewitt is keen on letting any of the teens near a ladder after Kevin almost fell off one last year, trying to show off for the girls."

Marge chuckled. "I forgot about that. We could ask David Martin to help. He was always willing to lend a hand in the past. Although I haven't seen him in church for a long time, and I'm surprised he got upset. I've never heard him utter a cross word to anyone."

"I don't know him well, but it surprised me too. We served on the church board together for a year. He replaced Carol Muncy when she had to resign. There were some heated discussions at a couple of meetings, but he always seemed pretty even-tempered."

Marge shrugged. "Maybe he doesn't like cops."

David scooped a shovelful of snow and pitched it aside. He'd cleared his own driveway before leaving for the community center gym this morning, but his neighbor, Bill Pender, could use a hand. He ran the shovel along the cement.

The front door inched open, followed by the screech of the screen door window edging along its track. Bill appeared, wearing a black turtle neck sweater and dark jeans. He spoke through the screen. "Hey, David."

"Morning, Bill."

"I appreciate you clearing that walk and—" A vigorous cough interrupted his words. He leaned forward and placed his hand over his mouth. The cough deepened. He braced against the door.

David anchored the shovel in a snowbank and hurried up the front steps. "Are you okay?"

Bill straightened some and extended his wrist in a wave. His cough continued, but he nodded his head. "Okay," he managed to utter. The coughing fit ended and he stood to his

CATHY'S CHRISTMAS CONFESSION

full height. "Days like this, that cold air gets to me. My lungs aren't so good anymore."

"You better take it easy, get back inside and rest."

"Ah, I been resting all night. Time to greet the day. As I was saying, thanks for clearing the walk and the driveway. Anita wants to go Christmas shopping today. I'd rather hold off until the roads are clear, but she'll probably get her way. She always does, willful woman that she is." His lips puckered into a pout. "Couldn't get by without her, though. Don't you go tell her I said that. She already has the upper hand around here."

David grinned, even though a pang of sadness stabbed his chest. "I don't mind getting some exercise and helping folks out at the same time." Anything to keep busy.

"You done any Christmas shopping yet?"

The question caught David off guard. "I don't have anyone to shop for."

UPS didn't deliver to Heaven. His fists tightened around the shovel. This time last year, he had scoured all the shopping hot spots in town, searching for unique gifts for his wife. How she delighted in unwrapping presents and watching him open his. Christmas music had filled their home from dawn until bedtime, lights twinkled from the walls, holly hung from the ceiling, and every surface that could displayed some type of Christmas knick-knack.

David had boxed up most of the holiday decorations and shipped them to his daughter in Denver. Michelle could use them in her ornate house. He had no place for such things in his small apartment, and no desire to decorate anyway.

Christmas music drifted through Bill's screen door. David caught only a few of the words. He didn't recognize the tune.

17

Probably a modern Christmas song performed by one of the country and western artists of the day.

Bill disappeared, then returned and opened the door. His poodle, Daisy, pranced down the steps, hesitated, and looked back at her owner.

"Go do your business, girl." The dog let out a low whine. When Bill motioned her away, the poodle trotted off into the snow. Bill stepped out onto the small porch. David was glad to see he had put on a jacket. "First year without your wife, isn't it?"

David inhaled and blew out a breath he could see in the cold. "Yeah."

"Tough break. Don't you have grandkids?"

David nodded. "Three. Two boys and a girl."

"Won't you shop for them?"

"I'll probably buy them a couple of little things, but I sent a check to my daughter. It's easier for her to pick out gifts than it is me." He flung more snow aside. "It was fun when they were little and I could buy toys. Now, with all these fancy tech gadgets they're into, the clothes they wear, I'd have no idea what to even look for."

Bill brushed snow off the wooden patio bench with a mittened hand and sat. "You know, there's always little kids you could buy toys for. Plenty of underprivileged kids would love gifts to open."

"When I was teaching, I used to wonder about certain students, what kind of Christmas they would have. I thought about buying a gift for some, but couldn't do it without showing favoritism. I never was much of a shopper. Heather did all the shopping."

Heather loved to shop. She always found the perfect gift

18

for everyone on her Christmas list. Wrapping and decorating the packages had been one of her favorite holiday activities. How he would miss the Christmas paper laid out on the dining room table, rolls of tape always being misplaced, bags of bows and ribbons, and silly little doo-dads she would tuck in among the trimmings.

Daisy padded up the walk and onto the porch. She lifted a dainty paw and shook the snow off. Bill chuckled. "Come on, girl. I'll let you back in where it's warm." He opened the door for the dog.

"I'm done here, Bill. Do you have any ice melt? This is still likely to freeze over."

"Yeah, right inside the garage. I'll hit the door open for you. Hey, thanks again."

"Any time. Glad to help."

"By the way." Bill twisted around to address David before heading into the house. "Heard tell there's a motorcycle toy run going to take place for underprivileged kids. Think they're organizing it over at the radio station. If you want to get into the Christmas spirit, you could buy some toys and donate them to that."

"Maybe."

Christmas spirit? He didn't have any.

CHAPTER 3

Cathy slipped into the closest parking spot she could find to the hardware store and killed the engine. She had written down the specifications for the headlight she needed on a used envelope and tucked it into her purse before leaving the house. Better to search for it out here than try to locate it once inside the store. She rummaged through what she referred to as her mini suitcase with no success.

She pulled a handful of assorted items out and laid them on the passenger seat. A small tube of hand cream, tissues, cosmetics mirror, comb, and an assortment of papers, but not the one she needed. She peeled off her gloves and separated the papers. Why did she keep this stuff? Old register receipts, folded up flyers for events that occurred months ago, a ticket to a school play she never attended, empty candy wrappers.

Frustrated, she gave up the search. The information was probably lying on her kitchen table at home. Hopefully someone in the store could help her with what she needed. She reached for her wallet. There. It jogged a memory. Sure enough, when she unclasped it, she found the envelope folded and pinched between a book of stamps and a ten-dollar bill. She stuck it in her jacket pocket.

A couple she knew from church exited a store, loaded down with sacks of merchandise. She stopped to chat with them for a moment, then moved on. A sudden gust of wind caught an elderly woman unaware. A long tube of Christmas wrapping paper slipped out of her hands, skittered down the street, and came to rest against a light pole.

"Oh, goodness gracious." The woman's eyes widened as she clasped her other parcels close. She tried to quicken her pace to chase the runaway item.

Cathy retrieved the roll of paper as the woman shuffled up behind her.

"My, my. That wind like to knocked me over. Thank you." She reached for the wrapping paper.

"It was a pretty good blast all right. Let me carry this for you. And these." Cathy slipped the sacks weighing down the woman's fragile arms into her grasp.

"Oh, my, thank you, Dear. How kind of you. I'm parked right down there. The blue Chevy." She pointed.

"This roll of paper is huge. You must have some big packages to wrap."

Despite a few missing teeth, a bright smile lit up the woman's face. "Yes, I bought my son and daughter-in-law a big screen TV set for Christmas. They love to watch the Denver Broncos and the Colorado Rockies. They'll be able to pretend they are right there where all the action is. John and his Missy are so good to me. I've been wanting to get them a special gift for a long while. Something they will enjoy after I'm gone. I finally saved the money."

"I'm sure they'll be thrilled." Cathy took the woman's arm

as she stepped off the curb. "How will you manage wrapping a gift that big?"

"My great granddaughter is coming over to help me tonight. I hope I can keep her from spilling the secret. She's so excited." The woman's eyes sparkled.

"Christmas secrets can be such fun."

"Yes, they can. Let me find my key and open the door for you." The woman fished in a deep pocket of her long coat and came up with a single key attached to a Denver Broncos keychain. She unlocked the driver's door, then reached over the back of the front seat to unlatch the rear door. Cathy hid her grin behind her hand. When was the last time she'd seen a vehicle with manual door locks?

Cathy deposited the wrapping paper and sacks in the back seat. Even though an older model, the car was spotless inside. She ducked out from the vehicle's interior. "You have one of the cleanest cars I've ever seen."

The woman's face beamed with pride. "My late husband bought this car brand new in 1993. A Caprice Classic. My son takes good care of it for me. It may be old, but it gets me where I need to go."

"That's amazing. Have a good day. God bless you." She turned to go, but the woman blocked her path. She clasped Cathy's bare hands between her blue cloth gloved palms before Cathy could thrust them into her pockets. Exposure to the frigid air had turned her skin red. She lamented her gloves lying in the front seat of her truck where she had left them. She didn't know she'd be making a detour before entering the hardware store.

"You're such a blessing. Now, I must have your name."

"My name?" Cathy blinked. "I'm Cathy. Cathy Fischer."

The woman placed her right hand across her heart, her left still firm in its grasp. "I'm Mrs. Maybelle Lovejoy. It's a delight to know you, Cathy Fischer." She displayed her endearing smile again. "May you have a Happy Jesus's Birthday!"

Cathy grinned. "A delightful way to say Merry Christmas, Mrs. Lovejoy."

Maybelle's laugh lines tightened and her expression turned serious. "You do know about Jesus, don't you?"

"Of course. I'm a church secretary."

Maybelle's intense gaze held Cathy in its grip. "Then introduce Him to others." The old woman squeezed Cathy's hand. "Share Christmas joy. Everyone needs to know who He is." She cupped her palm around Cathy's shoulder. "Way too many don't."

Cathy squirmed inside but didn't dare look away. She couldn't.

Maybelle's eyes softened. "Have a wonderful Merry Christmas."

"May your Christmas be blessed."

Maybelle's expression radiated joy. "It will be. I'm counting on it." She opened the car door and settled into the driver's seat. She cranked the window down and winked. "I'll be celebrating in style."

Cathy stood on the sidewalk in a daze and watched Maybelle's car until it disappeared around a corner. What had the old woman been trying to tell her? Introduce Jesus to others. Way too many people don't know about Jesus. What an odd statement. Everyone she knew did, didn't they? Where was she to find these people who didn't?

CATHY'S CHRISTMAS CONFESSION

DAVID ENTERED THE COMMUNITY CENTER EXERCISE ROOM, traded his snow boots for gym shoes, and turned on the treadmill. He usually ran outdoors, but winter held Christmas Ridge captive in a relentless onslaught of chilly winds and intermittent skiffs of snow. No point in taking the risk of breaking a leg on snow-packed roads and icy sidewalks. The community center with its treadmills offered a suitable alternative.

He warmed up with a leisurely two point five miles per hour walk and gradually worked up to five point two. He had enjoyed running from young boyhood, but his four years in the Air Force had taught him the true value of exercise. It kept his body in shape and his mind clear.

His doctor had assured him at his last physical that he was in great condition for a man approaching seventy. His lungs and muscles were strong, and his heart functioned at excellent capacity.

Amazing that the doctor had been unable to detect the gaping hole in the middle of that heart. Ten months ago today, he had held Heather's cold, pale hand as she took her last breath. His world had come to an abrupt halt in that moment when she had passed from this world to her eternal home.

Movement on the treadmill helped drain away the tension in his body but did nothing to relieve the ache in his soul. He was at an emotional standstill, waiting for meaning to filter back into his life.

David finished his routine with a ten-minute dumbbell workout. He grabbed a towel from his gym bag and wiped away sweat, then took a slug of water from his "#1 husband" water bottle, a gift from Heather last Christmas.

Last Christmas.

Her last Christmas.

He took a deep breath and descended the stairs two at a time.

Esther Matthews, the receptionist, called his name.

David turned and greeted her with a forced smile. "Morning."

"Don't morning me. You know what I want." She lifted an eyebrow. "I'm going to get it out of you if I have to twist your arm to do it."

David grinned. "Hard core mean today, huh?"

She pushed a clipboard across the counter. "Your signature. Right there." She tapped a polished fingernail against the first line on the sheet. "Time in, please."

"Yes, ma'am." He scrolled the information and handed the clipboard back.

She waved the same polished finger at him. "You know our attendance records play a big part in our funding." She pursed her red-coated lips. "You haven't signed in all week."

"I know. I have a thing about putting my signature on legal documents that may incriminate me. Or, to be honest about it, I just plain forget."

She smiled. "You're not the only one. Maybe I should put up a 'please sign in' notice at the back door. People sneak in and out all the time." Her tone turned serious. "How have you been, David?"

"I'm fine." The lie slipped out easily.

Esther shook her head. "You look a little rough. Are you getting enough sleep?"

"Sometimes."

"Eating okay?"

He patted his stomach. "Do I look malnourished?"

"I haven't seen you at church for quite a while." She furrowed her forehead. "How long has it been?"

"I haven't been back since Heather—" He looked at his feet and back to Esther. "The thought of attending church without her is just too hard."

"I understand, but David, don't neglect your soul."

David rushed to his Challenger, hopped into the vehicle, and took a deep breath. He sat for a long moment in the near empty parking lot. Glancing at his reflection in the rearview mirror, he jerked his head in shock. When was the last time he had taken a good look at himself? His eyes were sunken, and he'd sprouted a three days' growth of beard on his chin. Even his hair looked somewhat disheveled.

No wonder Esther had inquired as to his wellbeing. He looked like a convict on the run. This Christmas season held no joy for him, but he wouldn't let himself fall back into the tunnel of despair he'd driven himself into after Heather's death. He had to find a way out. This wasn't the man he wanted to be.

Certainly not the man Heather would have expected him to be.

CHAPTER 4

Cathy tapped on Pastor Hewitt's office door.

"Come in." His voice beckoned her with a welcoming tone.

He looked up with a smile of pleasant greeting. "Cathy, good morning. What can I do for you?"

"I'd like to talk to you if you have a moment, Pastor."

"Absolutely. Take a seat." He gestured to the cushioned gray sofa across from his desk. A ray of morning sunshine highlighted the floral pillow tucked against its arm. Pastor Hewitt put down his pen, leaned back, and clasped his hands in front of him.

"I want to share a concern about one of our members."

"Sure." He nodded. "There's a confidentiality issue if I've counseled the person, but you already know that. I'll try to help as best I can."

Cathy leaned back and hugged the soft pillow to her chest. "The person in question is David Martin. I don't know him well, but what little I do know—" she shook her head "—I feel like something's off with him lately."

Pastor Hewitt picked up a pen and rolled it between his thumb and forefinger. "David and Heather joined our church shortly after they arrived in Christmas Ridge, so they were already members when I started here. I believe you served on church board with him for a year, didn't you?"

She nodded. "That's how I know him. The only way I know him really."

"He was planning to serve the next term, but his wife was diagnosed with cancer. Her illness progressed rapidly. She died," he furrowed his brow, "I want to say around February." He hunched over his desk and consulted a write-in calendar. "Yes, her funeral was February seventh. He sent a note of thanks for the service, but he hasn't been back to church since. I visited him once. He gave me the impression I was interrupting something he had planned, so the next time, I made it a point to call. He told me he was fine and didn't need another visit. I've followed up a couple of times since, invited him to come in and talk, told him we miss him at Sunday services, but I haven't seen him."

Cathy explained about her encounter with David at the scene of her accident. "He wasn't rude to the police officer, but he was definitely perturbed. I remember him being so calm and even-tempered during our meetings.

"I can't say for sure, but I think I saw him in the hardware store. Seemed he was annoyed at the clerk for some reason. His behavior isn't lining up with what I thought I knew about him." She bit her lip. "Something doesn't add up, and I don't know if it's my business to interfere."

"Grief can do strange things to people. Have you prayed about it?" The pastor's prompting held no accusation.

"No. I haven't. Speaking of prayer, you and I have

30

CATHY'S CHRISTMAS CONFESSION

discussed ways God communicates with us. Sometimes through other people."

"Oh yes, and through His word."

"I had the most amazing encounter." Cathy leaned forward. "Do you know a lady named Maybelle Lovejoy?"

Pastor Hewitt shook his head. "Can't say as I do."

"She's probably about ninety years old. Still drives. I'd guess she has more spunk than people ten years younger. I only spoke with her for a couple of minutes, but she impacted me in almost a supernatural way. She asked me if I know about Jesus. When I assured her that I do and told her I'm a church secretary, it was like she laid a burden on me to tell everyone I know about Jesus." Cathy swallowed, remembering the depth of emotion Maybelle had elicited in her.

"It baffled me to hear her say that. I assume anyone I have a close association with does know about Jesus. The more I've thought about it, though," she lowered her eyes and stared at the floor, "the more I realize that may not be true at all. I'm not good at sharing my faith."

She returned her gaze to Pastor Hewitt. "My 'God bless you' sounds so—so trite at times. I know it has powerful meaning, but, well, I've been saying it automatically since I was a kid when somebody sneezes." She giggled then choked up. A tear slid down her cheek. "Hurting people need something more, and I don't know if I'm equipped to provide whatever it is."

Tears streamed down her face. She reached for a tissue and blotted them away.

Pastor Hewitt came around his desk and laid a hand on her shoulder. "Cathy, you're deeply moved for a reason. I believe God is calling you to something very special. You're right.

31

You're not equipped, but God equips the called. There are a multitude of hurting people out there, and like Mrs. Lovejoy said, many who don't know about Jesus."

He glanced out the window and nodded. "Look at this town. How many churches do we have here altogether? Five? If we were to add up our attendance at Christmas Ridge Community with that of all the other churches put together, the total wouldn't equal even twenty percent of the population. Where are all those other people? Why aren't they attending church? Do they know about Jesus? Do all of our members truly know?"

Cathy blew her nose, tossed the tissue in the trash can, and reached for another from Pastor Hewitt's desk. "You've given me some things to think about. Where do I find these people? How do I reach them?"

"You reach people every day in ways you may not even realize. A word of encouragement, a prayer, the cards you send out, the thoughts for the week you put in the bulletins. All of those little things mean so much. You may never know how much of an impact they have." Pastor Hewitt returned to his desk and rested his chin on his steepled palms. "You can't go out there and reach them all, but I believe God has laid a burden on your heart, perhaps to help David Martin or maybe someone else who may cross your path. If you can touch the life of one other person in a positive manner, you will have accomplished a great thing in life. Pray about it and wait on His good timing."

"Thank you, Pastor Hewitt."

He grinned. "I still wish you'd call me Tim."

"Sorry. This old lady is stubborn."

"You might be surprised to see how God can use your stubbornness."

When Cathy returned to the office, she prayed for guidance. *Please, Lord, help me find a way to reach out to those who need me.*

She opened a drawer and pulled out a stack of files. Copies of old newsletters, Sunday bulletins. Lists of hymns. Membership list. She glanced over the names.

One name jumped out at her. David Martin. Perhaps Marge was right. They could use his help Thursday night, and maybe he could use theirs.

Only one way to find out.

DAVID SCRAPED AWAY THE LAST OF HIS WHISKERS AND STUDIED his reflection in the mirror. Big improvement from the scroungy looking face that had stared back at him from his rearview mirror in the community center parking lot a couple of days ago. He had vowed not to let his personal appearance deteriorate again. He may be a wreck on the inside, but he needed to keep up the outward appearances of a person with a purpose.

He poured a cup of coffee and dumped a helping of cereal into a bowl. Focusing on the opposite wall as he ate, his thoughts wandered down the same path they had traveled for months now. If only Heather was here, they'd be sharing a hearty breakfast of bacon and eggs, maybe even homemade cinnamon rolls.

Heather wasn't here.

But he was.

There lay the stark reality of it.

He may not see it now, but he did have a future.

He placed his dirty dishes in the sink, all two of them. A wry smile twisted his lips. Heather had taught him well. No one would ever find dirty dishes piled up in his kitchen. She believed in washing dishes after every meal, and he'd kept up the practice, even when he knew the chances of anyone entering his home were highly unlikely.

She would be proud of him.

Or would she?

He had tucked the devotional booklets that arrived by mail into a drawer unread. He and Heather used to read a devotional together every evening. He missed those few minutes when they would discuss the short reading, study the scripture verse, and pray.

They had attended church every Sunday morning and participated in the social events held there. Heather, more outgoing than David, jumped right in when some committee needed assistance. She loved to decorate, cook, and help organize activities.

His phone chirped, pulling him out of his reverie. He hadn't received a call for quite some time. 'Church' flashed across the screen. Probably Pastor Hewitt. Should he accept the call? What could he say to the man? He held his finger over the screen for a moment, then swiped to answer. "Hello."

"David. This is Cathy Fischer."

"Cathy." David's voice registered his surprise. "How are you? Everything turn out okay after the accident?"

"I'm getting the headlight replaced in a few days. The body work will have to wait until after the holidays."

CATHY'S CHRISTMAS CONFESSION

"You can get by with a couple of dents. That light needs fixed so you can drive at night."

"Right." A pause ensued, then she stammered the next couple of words. "So— I called to find out—"

Why did she call? His curiosity piqued.

"How are you at climbing ladders?"

He blinked. Another surprise. "Pretty good, unless you ask me to climb up a roof with a steep slant. Why?"

"We're going to be decorating at the church Thursday evening and we could use your help. Tom Prescott was our climber last year, but he has a broken foot."

David hesitated. He hadn't been inside the church in so long. He'd made himself an outcast. "Well, I—I suppose I could come help."

He heard the smile in Cathy's voice. "You'd be welcome. I can assure you of that."

Would he?

"What time?"

"We'll see you around six?"

"OK. I'll be there."

David disconnected and took a deep breath. He hadn't stepped inside the church since the day of Heather's funeral. Could he do this? He belonged back at church. He knew it. He just hadn't been able to make himself attend a Sunday service. Perhaps this would be a step he could take. At least he would be busy. And the busier he was, the less time he had to think.

35

CHAPTER 5

Cathy pulled the top from a plastic tote and unpacked its contents onto a long table. "I called David Martin and invited him to help us decorate. I hope he shows."

"Do you think he will?" Marge raised her eyebrows.

"No way to tell, but I've been praying for him. I'm leaving it up to God to nudge him toward people who can help him. Whether that's us or not remains to be seen."

Marge opened a white box to reveal eight tiny glass angels nestled in a bed of velvet. "I forgot about these." Her eyes lit up. "Can't ever have enough angels at Christmas."

Cathy pulled one of the glass figures from the box and cradled it in her palm. "Exquisite." She studied the ornament with admiration. "I don't remember seeing these on the tree last year."

Marge turned one upside down. "This switch lights them up, and the colors change from red to orange to green to purple. Mrs. Wilson donated these a couple of years ago. If I remember right, we didn't have any batteries for them. I think we ordered some for this year, though." She picked up another box. "Yep, here they are."

Others drifted into the meeting hall and Cathy took the lead in giving directions. "Construction paper, glue, plastic scissors are on this table for the little ones to make paper chains." She pointed to the adjacent table. "Over here we have crayons and Christmas themed coloring books. We'll use the chains to decorate the tree in the nursery and the pictures will hang on the bulletin board. Ornaments are over here if you older kids would like to decorate this tree." She pointed to the large artificial tree standing in the corner.

The room buzzed with conversation and laughter as everyone became engrossed in their various activities.

Cathy and Marge separated the contents of the tote. Cathy stacked four identical boxes of red glass balls. "We have too many of these. We can give some away. This tinsel is still good." She kept up a running commentary of inventory, keeping her tone light as her anxiety heightened over David's absence. Had he decided not to come?

Marge motioned toward the door. "Here's our man."

Cathy breathed a sigh of relief and hurried to greet him. Before she could get across the room to David, one of the younger children ran up and hugged him. "Mr. Martin!"

David grinned. "Hi, Joey." He sauntered over to the busy table. "What are you all making?"

"Decorations for the tree in the nursery."

"I'm coloring a picture of Jesus in the hay," another young voice piped up. "That's where He slept after He got born."

The adults chimed in with welcoming greetings of "good to see yous" and "how have you beens."

Cathy came up beside him. "Hi. Glad you're here."

CATHY'S CHRISTMAS CONFESSION

"Sorry I'm late. I had to run a quick errand." He wore blue jeans and a dark blue crewneck sweater. Despite his casual dress and friendly demeanor, he looked as uncomfortable as a new student who had blundered into the wrong classroom.

"You're right on time. Marge and I are going through the decorations we've accumulated over the years." She directed him to their work station.

"Hey, David." Marge greeted him with a warm smile. "Want some ornaments to take home? We have plenty of extras." She swept her hand over the table.

He stiffened and shoved his hands in his pockets. "No, thanks. I probably won't decorate this year." He glanced around the room. "What did you need me to do?"

"Pastor Hewitt is around here somewhere." Cathy searched to think of something to say to help David relax. She was grateful when she heard Pastor Hewitt's voice.

"Right here." The pastor came up the basement stairs carrying a long cardboard box.

David rushed to help him navigate through the door with the ungainly carton.

"Thanks. It's not heavy, just awkward."

The two men eased the box to a table.

Pastor Hewitt offered David a friendly handshake. "Good to see you again. We've missed you around here."

David accepted the handshake, but his body remained tense. A muscle twitched along the length of his temple. Had Cathy made a mistake by inviting him here?

"I know I haven't been to church for a while, Pastor Tim. I—"

Pastor Hewitt held up his palm. "Hey, no excuses needed and no apologies expected. You've had to make some

39

adjustments. We all understand that. We just want to be here for you in whatever way you need us. We're grateful for your help."

David's facial muscles relaxed.

"I have a confession to make." Pastor Hewitt grinned. "I'm glad you're here because my number one fear is heights. Anything more than two inches off the ground and I get dizzy."

David crossed his hand over his heart, then extended his arm out in a gesture of acceptance. "Heights don't bother me in the least. Lead on."

Cathy observed the exchange with a critical eye from her work station.

Marge leaned in close. "What do you think?"

Cathy glanced back toward the two men. "At least he doesn't look like he's walked into a lion's den anymore. I think Pastor Hewitt is putting him at ease."

"Pastor Tim has a gift for making people comfortable."

Cathy watched David as he carried out the task the pastor assigned him. He moved with confidence and purpose up the first four rungs of the tall step ladder. Pastor Hewitt handed him a wreath.

"There should be a nail still there from last year," Pastor Hewitt said.

"I see it." David placed the green wreath, adorned with silver bells and a big red bow in the middle, on the nail. He leaned back and in again, repositioning the decoration until it was centered. "How does it look?"

"Perfect from here," Cathy called.

"Nice," Marge added.

David descended the ladder. "What's next?"

The evening progressed with an atmosphere of fun and merriment. David kept busy as he climbed up and down the ladder to loop greens along the walls.

"Next project is the tree in the sanctuary," Pastor Hewitt announced. "That's where we hang the Chrismons. David and I will be in there if anyone would like to join us."

Cathy waved. "Don't forget to come back for refreshments."

DAVID HELPED PASTOR TIM SET THE BOX OF CHRISMONS ON A rolling cart to move them into the sanctuary.

"Charlie Brooks put the tree up a couple of days ago. He knew we'd be decorating tonight. He does a lot of little things like that without being asked." The pastor opened the box. "I'm told these Chrismons have been in our church for many years."

"I haven't seen decorations like these in any other church I ever attended." David studied one of the white and gold objects. "Tell me about them."

Pastor Tim's face lit up. "The word Chrismon is a combination of the words 'Christ' and 'monogram.' Each one represents some facet of Jesus's life, some aspect of His ministry, and portrays the essence of His meaning to Christians.

"Take this one here." He chose one in the shape of a letter 'P' with an 'X' lying on its side across the stem of the 'P.' Two symbols hung from the arms of the 'X.' He pinched one symbol and then the other between his thumb and forefinger. "These are the first two letters in the word Christ in the Greek alphabet." He hung the Chrismon on the tree and reached for another.

"This one, the orb with a cross over it is a reminder that we in this world need Christ."

David picked up a Chrismon in the shape of a crown. "And this reminds us that Jesus is the King of Kings."

Tim nodded. "The white and gold colors are symbolic as well. White reflects Jesus's perfection, His purity, his innocence. The gold represents the majesty and glory of God. Did you know white symbolizes joy?"

"No. I didn't." David longed to experience Christmas joy this season. He should be filled with anticipation at the celebration of the Savior's birth. He'd always considered himself a good Christian, faithful in his religious practice and grateful for the gift of God's son.

He hung a few more ornaments, then stepped over to the nativity scene. Each piece, from Mary and Joseph leaning over the baby Jesus in His bed of straw, to the shepherds and animals hovering nearby, displayed exquisite detail. The ornate exhibit spanned a major portion of the area behind the altar. The scene it depicted brought a rush of emotion to David. Could the birth of the Savior bring joy back to his wounded heart?

Pastor Tim's voice pulled David out of his meditation. "A long-deceased member of the congregation hand-crafted this decades ago."

David cleared his throat. "Admirable work."

"Yes." Pastor Tim placed his hand on David's shoulder. "I know this is a difficult time of year for you. Remember that God loves you. He sees your pain. He sent His son to feed us, teach us, love us, heal us. Let Him do that for you, David. If I can help in any way, please come see me."

David swallowed the lump in his throat and nodded.

Did he know God loved Him? How deeply did he love God? The rote recitation of prayers didn't mean a thing if they didn't originate from the heart. When was the last time he'd even prayed at all?

He had neglected his faith these past months, and his indifference had taken its measure on his soul. A chasm had widened between himself and God. He had heard in sermons over the years that when hard times come and a person senses a distance from God, it's not God who pulls away.

David hadn't been pulling away.

He'd been running at full speed.

CATHY AND MARGE SET OUT CHRISTMAS PAPER PLATES AND napkins for refreshments. After the decorating was all done, everyone came together for punch and cookies.

David took a bite of cookie and wiped his lips with his napkin. "These are delicious. Snickerdoodles are one of my favorites."

"Cathy always brings the best cookies," Marge said.

She blushed and waved a hand. "Oh, goodness, it's the least I can do. I don't have the creative talent for decorating like you all do."

"Try the one with the chocolate kiss, Mr. Martin." Joey bounced up and down in his chair. "Mrs. Fischer calls them surprise cookies because they have peanut butter but you can't see it." The boy reached for one and bit off the chocolate candy on top.

"Last one, Joey," his mom admonished. "You've had plenty. You don't want to wake up with a bellyache."

The little boy's face fell. "Yes, Mom."

"Mr. Martin, come see the tree we decorated." Little Alicia came around the table and reached for David's hand. "We worked really hard."

"I'd love to."

The other young children gathered around him and led him to the nursery.

When he returned, he joined the conversation with an occasional comment, although Cathy noticed his demeanor was reserved. A deep sadness clouded his eyes. Had he enjoyed the evening?

Once parents left with the little ones, the teens sat at their own table engaged in animated chatter. Suddenly, the noise level in the room quieted.

David glanced at their table and back to Pastor Hewitt. "They're up to something." He spoke in a low tone and nodded toward the cluster of youth.

"Like what?" Cathy shot David a curious look.

"I don't know, but I've worked around kids enough to recognize the signs." He shrugged.

Pastor Hewitt grinned. "I'd guess something mischievous but not dangerous. Probably just planning a little fun."

The young people pushed back their chairs and sauntered over to the adults' table. "We're heading out, Pastor Tim," the oldest announced. Multiple thank yous were expressed for the enjoyable evening and refreshments.

"See you all Sunday. Thanks for your help."

CATHY'S CHRISTMAS CONFESSION

The four adults cleaned off the tables, gathered the trash, and put up the remaining snacks. They exited the back door and drifted toward the parking lot. A shout came out of the darkness followed by laughter. An object whizzed past Cathy. She turned toward David just in time to see a puff of snow land on his shoulder and dissipate to the ground.

"Over here, Mr. Martin," a voice shouted. David ran toward the sound and ducked behind a vehicle.

"Girls on this side," a female voice called. "It's the great snowball fight! Girls against guys!"

Marge and Cathy ran to the girls' side of the lot, shouting and laughing.

Shaylee, one of the teens, pointed to a cooler full of snowballs. "We prepared ahead of time." She giggled. "We've got our arsenal."

"Good thinking!" Marge chuckled. "Were you expecting this?"

"I overheard the guys talking when we met at the coffee shop earlier." Dark-haired Sarah spoke from behind a furry red mitten. "We sneaked off and got a few snowballs ready during the decorating."

"No head shots!" came a warning shout from Pastor Hewitt.

Snowballs pummeled the air with most of them missing their target and harmlessly hitting the ground. One of the boys stood up from behind the hood of a vehicle and Shaylee landed a snowball in the center of his chest. Finally, another boy waved his arms and declared defeat after a blast of the icy fluff exploded on his right leg and slithered into his boot.

Everyone said good-night with waves and merry shouts.

45

Cathy joined David at his vehicle. "David, I'm sorry you got caught up in all that. I was not expecting it."

He chuckled. "It was fun. I haven't been in a good snowball fight in years."

She sighed with relief. "I'm glad you had a good time." She tucked a strand of hair under her hat. "You've done me a favor twice now. I'd like to take you to breakfast tomorrow to say thank you if you're not busy."

"You would?" A bewildered look flitted across his face. "You don't need to do that. It did me good to get out around people again."

"I know I don't need to." She peered into his blue eyes. "I asked because I want to."

He glanced away from her gaze and drew a line in the snow with the toe of his boot. A boundary?

Perhaps this was a bad idea.

When he looked back up, a slight grin crawled across his features. "I'd enjoy that. I do get tired of eating with Me, Myself, and I. They don't make very good company."

She grinned. She hadn't crossed a line after all. "Shall we plan on 7:30 at Cookies 'n Cream?"

"Perfect."

CHAPTER 6

David paced outside Cookies 'n Cream, hands linked behind his back. The rich aroma of fresh brewed coffee and the sweet smell of tantalizing pastries floated out the door when a young couple entered the coffee shop. Cathy's invitation had flattered him, but David had spent a restless night wondering what motivation lay behind it. He hoped she wasn't planning to offer some kind of condolence to help him feel better. He'd heard enough of the 'I'm so sorry' and 'she's in a better place' and 'you'll get over it.' He didn't hear Cathy approach until she spoke softly behind him. "Good morning, David. Glad you could make it."

"Hi." He pasted on a smile. "I haven't been out to eat in quite some time. I couldn't pass up the opportunity." He held the glass door open for her.

They threaded their way past several occupied tables to a corner booth. "Looks like a popular place." She removed her jacket and scarf and took the seat facing the room, leaving him the window view.

"Shows they serve good food." David reached for a menu and offered her one.

"Thanks." Cathy opened the menu. "I haven't been here in so long. Any recommendations?"

"What's your preference? Healthy or sweet? Pastries on the left, breakfast burritos on the right. Coffee choices on the last page."

She studied the selections. "That cinnamon bun looks delicious, but so do the burritos. This combination will do it for me. Bacon, egg, potato, and cheese. Can't pass that up."

"Let me see if they've added anything since I was last here." David opened his menu and glanced at the pages, then replaced it into its holder at the side of the table. "I'll get the same as you, except with sausage instead of bacon. What kind of coffee would you like?"

"Dark roast with regular cream and sugar. I never did acquire a taste for all those fancy creamers and lattes and Frappa whatever they are. Can't pronounce half of it."

He grinned. "Same here. My wife liked the French vanilla creamer. I tried it once. Thought it tasted like somebody dumped root beer into my coffee."

She laughed.

The waitress arrived and David gave her their order.

He folded his hands and gazed around the shop, taking in the Christmas decorations, the low chatter among the customers, the Christmas music in the background. So much holiday spirit, but he felt like an intruder looking in on it all. "The last time I was here was with my wife." His face heated. He unfolded his napkin from his silverware and smoothed it into his lap. "I'm sorry. I shouldn't have mentioned it."

CATHY'S CHRISTMAS CONFESSION

Cathy's eyes softened with compassion. "Why not, if she's on your mind? Tell me about Heather."

He blinked. "What do you want to know?"

She gave him an inviting smile. "Whatever you'd like to tell me."

David folded his arms on the table and leaned in toward Cathy. "Heather was strong, sensitive, smart. She loved music and art and she had the biggest heart I've ever known. She was always giving something to someone or donating to a cause or—"

He stopped and stared past Cathy, visualizing his wife as though she had just walked into the room. "Heather never went anywhere until she was dressed impeccably from head to toe, including makeup and jewelry." He smiled. "She wouldn't even go outside to get the mail without her makeup. She was a lovely woman." He looked full at Cathy. "You knew her, didn't you?"

"Not well. I knew who she was because I'd seen her with you at church. I never served on a committee with her. Her talents were much different from mine, what little talent I have for anything." She snickered. "I don't have a lot to offer when it comes to decorating and planning. We spoke a few times is all. You're right. She was a beautiful woman."

"Heather could be haughty at times. She was born into an affluent family and there's no doubt her parents spoiled her, but deep inside beat the heart of a servant. She made me feel like the most important man in the world."

Cathy held his gaze for a long moment. "To her, I'm sure you were."

"Thank you for saying that."

49

Their food arrived. They spent the next few moments in silence as they stirred cream and sugar into their coffee.

David reached for his fork.

Cathy had bowed her head. Of course. She was probably offering a blessing. He put the fork down and waited.

When she glanced up again, her cheeks filled with a pink tinge. "Marge and I usually say a quick prayer when we eat together."

"I could use prayers. Heaven knows I haven't said enough of them myself lately."

"Well, in that case." She bowed her head again.

David did the same.

"Father," she prayed in a low tone, "we are two people who need You. We thank you for Your presence, we thank You for this food, and we ask Your blessing. In Jesus's name. Amen."

He picked up his fork and gave Cathy a sheepish grin. "I forgot I was eating with a church secretary."

She laughed, then her face turned serious. "I hope that wasn't awkward for you."

"We never did pray in public, but I'm okay with it. As much as I am with any prayer right now." He shrugged. "God and I haven't been on speaking terms lately."

"I'm sure you have your reasons."

Grateful she didn't press him on the issue, he took a bite of food.

"Heather kept me on track on that score. We used to read a devotional and pray together every evening. She'd be ashamed to see how I've neglected that aspect of my life."

"You miss her a lot." She sampled her burrito. Her eyes lit up. "This is good."

CATHY'S CHRISTMAS CONFESSION

"Like I'd miss my right arm."

"This is your first Christmas without her. You were married how many years?"

"Forty-eight. We got married right out of high school."

"That's a long time. Suddenly, you're without the woman who's been with you most of your life."

He nodded. "How long has it been for you?"

"Everett died two years ago this coming January."

"So, you're over the worst of the grief by now." He looked away and twisted his wedding band with his thumb. "I suppose I should be moving on, but I can't seem to get out of this rut I'm in."

Cathy picked up her napkin, wiped her mouth, and looked at him intently. "David. I don't know that we ever get over our grief. A couple of days ago in the hardware store, I had a near meltdown standing in front of a bin of nails. Of all the stupid things. A memory flashed across my mind of Everett buying screws and nails, how I used to get so annoyed waiting for him to pick what he wanted, and here came the tears. Totally unexpected."

Relief washed over him. "I get sentimental over the silliest things. Her favorite towel when I do the laundry. A coffee mug she always used with a chip in it." He shook his head. "Such insignificant things when she was alive. Now they mean the world to me.

"I still have her clothes packed away in boxes. I was thinking just the other day how selfish that is. Someone out there could use them." He waved toward the window.

"It was well over a year before I even started sorting things out to give away. I still have some of Everett's clothes. A jacket way too big for me. A hat I'll never wear. A box of

51

handkerchiefs his sister sent him for his birthday years ago that he never opened. I may hold on to those things for the rest of my life."

They ate in comfortable silence.

Audrey, the shop's owner, refilled their coffee cups. She tapped David's shoulder. "Hey, stranger, we haven't seen you in here for months."

"I know. It's been a while. Ever since Heather—" His voice faltered. "The places we went together. Just not the same."

"I understand. We were so sorry to hear about Heather." Audrey placed a comforting hand on his arm. "She was a sweet lady."

David clasped her hand. "Thank you. She loved your cherry turnovers." He remembered his manners. "Audrey, do you know Cathy Fischer? She's—"

Cathy jumped in. "Nice to meet you, Audrey. David and I know each other from church."

"Pleasure to have you here." Audrey nodded with a grin.

"My husband and I ate breakfast at your shop a couple of times. We lived out of town, so we didn't get here much. I've seen you but didn't know your name. You have a lovely shop. The burrito is wonderful. Crisp bacon, fluffy eggs, plenty of cheese."

Audrey beamed. "Thank you. Anything else I can get for you?"

They both shook their heads.

"I may leave with a cinnamon bun to go," Cathy said.

"Great. Let me clear these out of your way." She collected their empty plates.

David added more sugar to his coffee, then rested his arms

out in front of him on the table. "Cathy, this is good for me, to talk to someone who knows how I feel. I've kept so much sadness inside for all this time."

She brushed his hand. "I can sympathize, but I truly don't know how you feel. I'm sure your marriage was very different from mine. Your feelings relate to your memories of your relationship with Heather. Moments you can't share with someone else. They're treasures for you and you alone."

"You sound like you can see into my soul."

"Believe me. I can't." She smiled. "I can only imagine what might be there, but your soul belongs to God."

He grunted. "You can be sure He sees a lot there he doesn't want to see."

"That's true of all of us. Isn't that what Christmas is all about? The gift of a Savior?"

David recalled his thoughts in the sanctuary the previous evening. "The real meaning of Christmas should be more important than any hardship we're going through. I've lost touch with the joy." He slumped his shoulders and stared into his coffee cup.

Cathy tapped her fingernails against her coffee cup. "I've been thinking of ways to share Christmas joy this year. Maybe we can help ourselves by helping someone else. Adopt a needy family and offer assistance with gifts for the kids or something."

"Let me know if you come up with anything. It can't hurt." David shrugged.

After a long moment, she picked up the conversation. "I remember my first Christmas without Everett. It was lonely and cold because I made it that way. I withdrew from everyone and everything Christmas. I resented the joy of the season because I was angry that no one else was as miserable as me. It was selfish, and I later learned there were a lot of people in far worse situations than I." She finished her coffee, then bent her elbow on the table and rested her chin in her palm.

"Don't let that happen to you. Get involved. Find things to do. Go to the community center and see what they have to offer there. It's only a few bucks a year to join, and I've learned there are activities for many different interests, all age groups. I always wanted to learn how to knit, so now I'm in a knitting class. I wouldn't recommend that for you." She chuckled. "We even started a Scrabble Club."

"I haven't played Scrabble in years. That was a favorite at one of the foster—" He stopped short. His face flushed. "When I was a kid."

"We're trying to get up a team game, but so far, there's only three of us. A young couple I met at the library a few months ago and myself. Would you like to join?"

Her eager expression captivated him.

"I may just do that. When do you meet?" resume

"Monday evening at six. Upstairs, second room on the right. Yay!" She clapped her hands, and for a moment she looked several years younger.

"Don't think you're getting any winner for a partner. My thing is numbers. I'm a terrible speller."

She grinned. "Then you'll make the perfect competitor."

He glanced at his cell phone. "I need to be going. I promised a neighbor a ride to a doctor's appointment. I can't thank you enough for this. By the way, breakfast is on me." He stood and slipped on his jacket, then stepped over to help her with hers.

"No, I asked you."

He leaned close. "Don't make a scene. It's my pleasure."

"Thank you." She wrapped her scarf around her neck. "Let me leave you with this thought. A wise friend shared this with me when I was where you are now. Keep a daily routine to cherish the past, but seek new challenges to embrace the future."

CHAPTER 7

Anxious anticipation gripped Cathy. Would David show up at the Monday Night Scrabble Club? She dared not mention his possible appearance in case he didn't come. She had to admit the thought of seeing him again caused her heart to skip a beat. Their breakfast conversation the previous week had revealed his deep hurt and loneliness. What a blessing to relieve some of that desolation for him.

She made light conversation with the other players, Donna and Dennis Walker, even though her stomach was doing flip-flops. Would she be more nervous if he did join them or if he didn't? She turned over the letters and scrambled them for the first game. Slowly. Deliberately. Methodically.

A soft knock sounded at the door. Cathy took a sharp intake of breath as David walked into the room with a tentative stride. He wore the same expression as the day he arrived at the church to decorate, as though questioning whether he belonged.

Cathy stood and motioned him to a chair. "David, meet Donna and Dennis Walker."

"Hey, David." The two men reached across the table and shook hands. "Good to see you again."

"You two know each other?" Cathy's tone showed her surprise.

Donna nodded. "We three. David helped us with our kitchen remodel last year when we ran into a water damage problem. He's a wonderful handyman."

"Saved us a lot of headache and expense. We're still grateful."

"How about that. Three D's and a C." Cathy's neck heated. What a silly comment, but David picked up on it right away.

He eased into the chair next to hers. "But your C is worth more than a D."

She tapped him playfully on the shoulder. "Watch out, guys. He told me he wasn't much of a Scrabble player. I think he's been fooling. We're going to sweep you."

All four chuckled as they each chose a letter to determine the first player. David thought Cathy had won with a "U,' but Donna set him straight.

"The rules say the closest letter to 'A' starts first."

He deferred to Cathy. "Ladies first, always. Agreed, Dennis?"

"Absolutely."

"You men are so noble." Donna tittered. "It's refreshing."

They all chose their seven letters. Cathy scrunched up her forehead as she studied her picks. "OK, just to clarify, we're playing teams, right? So, David can help me?"

"Agreed," Dennis said.

"I think that's the way it should go," Donna added.

David leaned over to see Cathy's letters.

V-X-M-B-R-I-J

She clapped a soft victory clap and separated out four letters.

BRIM

David shook his head and picked out a different combination.

JIB

She frowned. "Only three letters to start the game?"

"Do you want twenty-four points or sixteen?"

"Okay, you have a point."

Donna groaned. "Starting off with a 'J' and a 'B'? Really? Talk about a cutthroat game." She added an 'A' and an 'R' to the 'J' for a score of ten. "I don't even get to use the double word square. I always thought that was unfair."

"Aw, poor baby!" Dennis chuckled. "Don't worry, sweetheart. They got the jump on us, but we'll catch up."

David shared a view of his letters with Cathy.

Q-W-C-E-E-O-O-P

Cathy separated out O-P-E to add to the R.

"Just a suggestion. It's your turn." She sat back as David leaned over his rack.

"Hold on a minute." He studied the letters and glanced back at the board. "How about this?" He spelled out C-O-O-P-E. "Before the 'R.'"

She nodded and he placed the letters on the board.

Donna raised her eyebrows. "Inadmissible. Proper noun. Person's name."

"Nope." David put on a smug grin. "Look it up. It's a profession. Someone who crafts or repairs barrels or casks."

"All right." She laughed. "That's why I like this game. I learn something new all the time."

An hour later, Donna and Dennis held the lead with a

thirty-five-point advantage. Cathy perused David's rack with deep concentration. She broke into a triumphant smile and bounced on her chair as she rearranged his letters.

"We've got it!" David laid the tiles on the board with a flourish.

JACUZZIS.

Cathy slapped her hand on the table. "Those blanks don't count for anything, but they sure do come in handy. All seven letters, so that's an extra fifty points."

Donna and Dennis's mouths fell open. "I don't believe it." Donna laughed and turned to her husband.

"That's some finale. You whipped us good," Dennis added.

"That's my partner." David gave Cathy a high five.

A tingle ran down her arm as he slapped her palm. His bright smile warmed her heart. It felt good to bring a bit of sunlight into his life.

"Time for cookies and punch." Donna stood. "Everybody in?"

"What kind of cookies?" Dennis asked.

"Ha! As if you're choosy." Donna batted her husband's shoulder. "I've never seen you turn down something sweet, let alone cookies from Cathy's house."

Cathy went to a side cabinet and pulled down a plastic container, along with paper plates and napkins. She opened the top and peered into the container as she crossed the room. "Looks like we have ginger snaps and a few of the chocolate surprise left." She placed the treats in the center of the table.

"I'll go get the punch." Donna breezed out the door and came back carrying a half-full gallon jug of cherry punch. She retrieved four tall red paper cups and filled three, then looked at David. "Would you like punch? We also have bottled water."

"The punch is fine. Thanks."

"I remember when you were working at the house, you slammed down quite a few bottled waters. I thought maybe you were one of those health nuts who abstains from sugar intake."

He laughed. "Water when I'm exercising or working, but I'm as much of a sucker for that sweet liquid energy as the next guy." He reached for a chocolate cookie.

Cathy brushed David's hand as he withdrew the cookie from the container. "Let me caution you, these have peanut butter, just in case you're allergic."

"I know. Joey clued me in at the church decorating party." His face took on a pensive look. "I've always loved peanut butter, but I could never have it in the house. Heather was severely allergic. Even the smell of it would cause her acute distress."

"Oh, I'm sorry." Cathy searched for the right words. "Food allergies must be so difficult to deal with. If I take peanut butter cookies anywhere public, I make sure to label them clearly for that very reason. I'd never forgive myself if I was the cause of someone else getting sick."

"Or dying," Donna said.

Cathy cringed inwardly. Why did that word have to come up David's first night here when he was so sensitive to the concept of death? She shot Donna a look, but it was lost to her animated friend. Didn't Donna know how fragile David was about the subject?

Donna prattled on. "We had a kid in high school who almost died when she took a bite out of a peanut butter and jelly sandwich at lunch time. She almost quit breathing. The weird thing," Donna continued, "is that she never had a problem with peanut butter before. She always ate the peanut butter cookies they had for dessert."

Cathy leaned forward. "I've heard of that, people developing an allergy when they never had one before."

"Heather wore an alert bracelet." David pried the chocolate kiss off his cookie with his fingernail and popped it into his mouth. "Her parents discovered her allergy when she was quite young."

"That's scary." Dennis took a sip of punch and reached for another cookie. "Now I'm going to be paranoid every time I eat peanut butter, afraid I'll drop dead."

Donna kissed her husband on the cheek. "You don't have a thing to worry about, my love. When do you ever eat that I'm not right there with you? Heaven forbid you should fix a meal on your own." She chuckled. "And peanut butter isn't the only food to be careful of. Shellfish, milk, eggs, tomatoes can all cause an allergic reaction. Some people even have allergies to celery and potatoes. The victim can develop a skin rash or hives all the way up to swelling of the throat. Sometimes it's a belly ache."

Dennis's lips twisted with amusement as he gazed at his wife with admiration. "Well, I declare. Thank you for that valuable information, Doctor Walker."

Laughter erupted from David.

Donna's face turned scarlet. "The only reason I know all that is because I read an article about it the other day."

Cathy grinned. "It's all right, Donna. We're all grateful that you imparted your knowledge to us." She flashed a smile

CATHY'S CHRISTMAS CONFESSION

across the table. Had all this talk of illness and death soured the evening for David?

"Anyone want another cookie?" Donna asked.

"They were very good, but I've had enough." David cleaned crumbs from his mouth with his napkin.

"Better put them up." Dennis plucked another ginger snap from the plastic bowl, broke it in half, and took a bite. "Leave 'em here and there won't be any left for the next group that meets in this room."

Cathy stored the cookies away, Donna took the punch to the kitchen, and the men cleaned off the table and disposed of the trash.

"Since we've decided not to meet again until after the holidays, I guess this may be my last opportunity to wish the two of you a Happy Jesus's Birthday." Cathy flashed a grin at her two friends.

Curious glances darted between Donna and Dennis. They both turned to look at Cathy. Donna's face heated and Dennis shuffled his feet, then cleared his throat. "We don't give much thought to the religious part of the holiday."

"We play up Santa and go for the gift giving to the kids in a big way." Donna offered a weak smile.

"And we donate toys to those boxes they put out in the stores. This year, we picked out—what, Hon—five or six toys and donated them to the toy run." Dennis gripped the back of a chair, looking smug.

"That's admirable." David spoke in a quiet, measured voice. "But there's a lot more to Christmas than that."

Donna waved a dismissive hand. "Neither of us grew up in a church, so we don't know much about all that stuff."

"Gift giving is a lot of fun and I imagine it's a really

exciting time for kids, but the most important thing is the gift God gave to us." Cathy emphasized the last word. "He sent us His son, Jesus, a gift that can never be surpassed by anything we could ever do for each other here on earth."

She was about to say more when David picked up the thought. "Jesus, the very son of God, humbled Himself to enter this world as a helpless infant. He could have come down from Heaven escorted by a thousand angels if He chose to do that, but instead, He showed His love for us by living among us and showing us how to live.

"He came to forgive our sins so we can have a relationship with God, go to Heaven and be with Him forever." David swept his arm out in a wide arc. "All of those who believe in Him, who believe Jesus is God's son, will be together in Heaven someday."

Donna looked at her husband in wonderment. "You mean, we could see our Lettie again?"

A look of hope crossed Dennis's features. "I—I don't know."

"Who's Lettie?" Cathy dropped her gaze to the table. "I'm sorry. I didn't mean to pry."

"No, it's fine. Lettie is our daughter. Leticia. We lost her at three months old. She was born before we moved to Christmas Ridge, before Paisley and Phillip. We just never mentioned it to anyone here." A tear shimmered down her cheek. "We didn't know about any of that. We just always thought Christmas was for kids and partying and having fun. It's a little embarrassing." Donna grabbed a strand of her long hair and tossed it over her shoulder.

Cathy swallowed around the lump in her throat. "Believe me, I learned something here tonight. I just assumed everyone knew about Jesus, but how is a person to know if no one ever tells them? Do either of you have a Bible?"

They both shook their heads.

"I'll get you one. I have several at my house. There are so many more wonderful things you need to know about Jesus."

David gripped Dennis's shoulder. "We'd welcome you at our church. Community Church on the corner of Pine Street and Second."

Cathy's heart hitched. Our church? Was David considering attending services again?

"We might plan to do that. Can we bring the children?" Donna's brow furrowed.

"Most definitely. Our number of kids has dwindled, but we have an excellent Sunday school teacher." Cathy zipped her jacket as they moved down the hall.

Dennis shook David's hand at the main entrance. "Good to have you here tonight, man. And thank you. Hope you come back."

"I probably will. Have to give you and Donna a chance to win a game."

They drifted toward the parking lot, the two men continuing their conversation. Cathy couldn't catch more than a few words here and there, but David's "be glad to help" came across loud enough for her to hear. Good.

Cathy and Donna trailed behind the men until Donna gripped Cathy's arm and jerked her to a standstill. She put her lips close to Cathy's ear. "So, are you two a couple?"

Taken aback by the question, Cathy reacted with a vehement "What? No!" She covered her mouth with her hand when she realized how loud her voice sounded in the cold, still air. The men seemed not to have noticed.

65

"No," she repeated more quietly. "I asked David to join us tonight because he needs socialization to help him through the Christmas season. The first since his wife passed. I remember what that was like." Better not tell Donna they had eaten breakfast together. She'd have them engaged by morning if she knew. "I'm hoping he gets comfortable with people again so he'll rekindle his old friendships or develop new ones."

Donna's piercing gaze made Cathy squirm inside. She looked away and studied the two men. Dennis gestured with his hands and David leaned against the Walkers' SUV. He nodded as though in agreement with what Dennis was saying. Two guys making plans for a project together.

The sight delighted Cathy. She silently chastised herself for her previous anxiety. If she had trusted the nudging that had prompted her to invite David to join them this evening, she wouldn't have let her stomach tie up in knots the way it had.

She looked back at Donna to see a silly grin spread across her face. "He likes you."

Cathy shuffled her feet. "I like him, too, but I don't mean like him, as in *like* him. Not like *that*." A nervous laugh escaped and she rushed on. "He's just an acquaintance who needs support through a tough time. That's it."

Donna put a hand on her shoulder. "Ok. I get it. I won't say a word."

After the Walkers left the parking lot, David fell in beside Cathy and walked her to her truck.

"I sure didn't anticipate that conversation." She pulled her collar up against the wind. "I've been playing Scrabble with those two for six months now and just assumed they were Christians. Thank you for jumping in there with me."

CATHY'S CHRISTMAS CONFESSION

"I was glad to do it. We don't talk about faith near as much as we should. I'm proud of you for taking the initiative."

She dug her key out of her pocket and hit the switch to unlock her door. Before she could open it, David did the honors for her. "Thank you. I'm not used to this kind of service."

His tone turned serious. "Every woman should be."

Her face flushed. "I'm not implying that Everett wasn't a gentleman. He was." She looked away for a brief moment, then back to David. "We lived in a world where most people stood on their own two feet and demonstrated a great deal of self-reliance, male and female." When a disturbed look crossed his face, she wished she could take back the words. "He was cut from a different cloth is all. Fiercely independent. I don't mean to imply that you—" She took a deep breath. How could she make such a mess of a simple statement?

He caught her gloved hand in his. "Thank you." He ran his thumb along the length of hers. She wished the thickness of the wool gloves they wore didn't hinder their contact. "Thank you for the enjoyable breakfast last week. Thank you for the fellowship this evening. Thank you for caring."

"I—I—it was an enlightening evening," was all she could manage to stammer.

"Until next time. Good night."

Suddenly, her jacket felt much too warm, even in the near zero air. David continued to hold her hand as she stepped on the running board and wriggled into the driver's seat. It was all she could do to squeak out a "goodnight."

God, don't let me mess this up. I'm just supposed to help. Right?

67

CHAPTER 8

David tossed two packages of pop tarts into his grocery basket.

"Breakfast of champions?" He turned at the sound of a voice, one he had come to recognize by now. Cathy leaned over her grocery cart and studied him with an inquisitive grin and raised eyebrows.

"Hey, a guy needs a break from dry cereal every now and again. Give me some credit. They're cinnamon." He glanced toward her cart.

"This is true. One of the top spices to boost the immune system against flus and viruses."

"And cancer." His voice flattened. "Heather used lots of cinnamon, took turmeric regularly, ate healthy foods. None of it helped. Maybe we initiated all those interventions too late."

She clasped his arm. "I'm sorry. I didn't mean to—" She stopped.

He narrowed his eyes. "You have nothing to apologize for. I brought up the word cancer. Not you."

"It must have been such a difficult time for you." She stepped away and clutched her shopping cart.

"Life is tough sometimes." He shuffled his feet. "I must move on. Don't want to miss out on the most desirable frozen dinners. There might be a run on them, you know."

"Tell me you're joking. You don't subsist on those things?" She extended her hand toward the pop tarts. "And them?"

He shrugged. "They're easy to prepare, require only silverware, and—" He gazed off as though seeking another advantage.

"—and probably packed with all kinds of hidden stuff that isn't good for you." Her eyes narrowed. "Are you one of those men who can't boil water without burning it?"

He hung his head in mock shame. "Guilty."

She bit her lip. "Listen, I have an idea. You did a wonderful job decorating at the church the other night. If you're willing to come to my house and hang Christmas lights, I'll fix you a real meal."

"You'd do that for me?" She certainly was a kind person.

She waggled a finger in front of him. "Not without a price. I want those lights up on my roof. I can't climb a ladder anymore, but it's definitely part of your skill set."

"Small price to pay for a real meal. I am a terrible cook."

"Don't get your hopes up too high, but it will be at least a step above processed food. What's your favorite meal?"

He grinned. "Surprise me. Make something you like and don't go to a lot of fuss on my account." He leaned toward her. "I trust your judgment."

She chuckled. "You may end up regretting that." She pursed her lips. "Any dietary restrictions?"

"None. And you know I love peanut butter. Just sayin', in case you should have a cookie or two lying around."

An impish smile spread across her face. "That settles that. PB&J it is."

He laughed.

"Shall we plan on tomorrow evening? I'm about three miles out past the radio station, the only house out there on the left for miles. You can't miss it. Say around three-thirty? You can string the lights before it gets too dark."

"I'll be there."

"What do you think, Horace? What should we feed David tomorrow evening?" Cathy spoke to her Siberian husky sprawled out on the kitchen floor as if he were a human companion capable of expressing an opinion.

The dog lifted his head, appraised her with a lazy look, and lay back down.

"Some help you are." She pulled out the recipe book she hardly ever used and scanned through the yellowed recipe cards and scraps of paper filed helter-skelter within. She hadn't followed an actual recipe since Everett's death. Her food choices had become so routine and repetitious that she didn't need recipes. A rotating fare of salads, sandwiches, meat and potatoes on occasion, or take-out.

Her phone played its incoming call chime. Marge's name flashed across the screen.

"Hey, Marge, what's up?" Something was always up with Marge, so Cathy had grown accustomed to answering her friend's calls with the question.

"Cathy, can you bring cookies to knitting club next week? I know you always have a stash of them in your freezer. Do you have any pfeffernusses? If not, how about the chocolate chip?"

"I'll see what I can do." Cathy made a mental note to check her cookie supply in her garage chest freezer. "I need your advice. Horace is no help whatsoever. He's worse at answering me than Everett was."

Marge chuckled. "You and that dog."

"I've made a deal with David Martin. He's going to come out and string outdoor Christmas lights for me tomorrow evening in exchange for a meal. Any ideas what I should fix?"

"Spaghetti." Marge's response was immediate.

"You're kidding." Cathy tapped her chin with her fingertips. "Now that you mention it, that might not be a bad idea. I could prepare the sauce in the morning in the crockpot before I leave for work. Then I wouldn't be in a rush when I get home."

"Absolutely. Your recipe is unique. Cathy Fischer's amazing Mexican spaghetti. You know how much my Bob loves it."

Cathy laughed. "Hardly unique. All I do is dump a can of chile into a basic spaghetti sauce recipe. It's not a big secret."

"Maybe not, but I don't know of anyone else who makes it that way. Don't forget to use the thin pasta."

"Noted." Cathy frowned. "I probably better go buy a new package. The one I have is pretty old. I haven't fixed spaghetti in so long. I don't want to find out it's got bugs. That would be embarrassing."

"I'll say." Marge's voice lowered. "After all, they say the secret to a man's heart is through his stomach. If you've progressed to inviting him over, you don't want to court disaster."

"It's not like that. I'm just trying to get him involved in doing things again, keep his mind off his grief over the Christmas holiday. After all, we're supposed to reach out as Christians to those who are hurting, aren't we? Just like you did for me. That's all I'm doing here."

"Uh-huh." Cathy could hear the amusement in Marge's voice. "How ironic that the person you chose to reach out to happens to be a handsome widower with a charming personality. Are you sure there's not an ulterior motive?"

Cathy felt a moment of indignation at her friend's insinuation, although she was grateful Marge couldn't see her face flush. "Definitely not. I would never try to take advantage of David's vulnerability. He's still deeply grieving the death of his wife. The last thing on his mind right now is beginning a relationship. He needs someone who understands his pain and can help him through it." Her explanation tumbled out in a rush. She glanced at the kitchen wall clock. "I better get to the grocery before it closes if I'm going to prepare this in the morning."

Marge's tone turned serious. "I'm proud of you, Cathy. You have a heart for others. Be careful, though. I don't want to see you hurt."

Just what did she mean by that?

CATHY RUSHED HOME FROM WORK. THE SMELL OF SPAGHETTI sauce wafted from the kitchen and permeated the house.

Horace greeted her at the front gate with his usual round of tail wags and tongue licks to her cheeks. "Hi, boy. I missed you."

Cathy hung up her coat and other outerwear in the hall closet, kicked off her boots, and checked on the spaghetti sauce. She sampled a spoonful. The savory tomato taste, tender pieces of hamburger, and just the right combination of spices teased her tongue.

What if David didn't like Italian food?

Stop it!

She'd never know. He was too much of a gentleman to protest.

She glanced at the clock. Two-thirty. She changed clothes and was about to head out to the garage to retrieve the boxes of Christmas lights when the stove hood caught her attention. It was filthy. When was the last time she had bothered to clean it? She grabbed a rag and some degreaser and went to work.

Next came the window sill. It, too, needed attention. She should mop the floor, but no time for that. She swept it, wiped up the visible coffee spills, and called it good.

What to fix besides garlic bread? The meal needed a little something else. Ah. Green salad. She peeled off some lettuce leaves, added sliced cucumber, a few slivers of green pepper, and black olives.

Horace scratched at the door. She let him in and caught his face in her palms. She looked into his eyes, one dark brown, the other pale blue. "Now, Horace, we're having company tonight. I want you to be on your best behavior." The dog trotted to the middle of the living room floor and rolled on his back with legs pointed toward the ceiling. Cathy knelt beside the big canine and ran her palm up and down his soft belly fur. "Horace, your mom's a nervous wreck."

Butterflies danced around in her stomach. Had this been a good idea?

She sank into her cushioned living room chair and took a deep breath. *Lord,* she prayed. *Please let David and me enjoy this evening, this meal. Help me to show him how much You love him. Help me show him the way to a Happy Jesus's birthday.*

CHAPTER 9

David's nostrils twitched with the tantalizing smell of tomato sauce when he stepped out of his vehicle. The next thing that drew his attention was the barking of a dog. Judging from the ferocity of the bark, a very large dog. He hesitated until Cathy appeared in the doorway.

"Come on in," she called. "He won't bite."

Sure.

David moved cautiously toward the house and up the front steps. The dog, no longer barking, stood next to Cathy with his tail wagging.

"David, meet Horace."

To David's surprise, the dog extended a paw in a handshake. He took the furry paw in his palm and looked at Cathy in wonder. "The way he was barking when I pulled up, I thought I'd have to give an arm to get in the door." The dog withdrew his paw and padded into the living room, where he lay down on a rug in front of the couch.

"I've trained him to carry on that way until I tell him it's okay. He's my watchdog."

"I'll say. I wouldn't want to come around if you're not here." He chuckled and turned toward the direction of the delicious smell. "Italian something?"

"Spaghetti. I hope you're okay with that."

He clapped his hands. "I love it. I think deep in my family tree lies Italian ancestry."

Cathy grinned. "Good. I set the lights out here on the porch. I'd like them to go along the roof like this." She indicated her intent with a sweep of her hand. "Up to the peak and back down the other side."

"No problem. I see you have a long ladder out there. That should do it."

By the time David had finished stringing the lights, the pasta was ready.

Cathy dashed outside to admire the festive addition to her house. "Thank you so much. They look wonderful. I haven't had lights up for a couple of years now." She shivered. "Let's get inside and eat. It's cold out here."

David relinquished his coat and glanced around the living room. A fire crackled in a fireplace, giving the room a toasty feel. A photo on top of the mantle of a young woman and an older man caught his attention. Cathy and her father years ago? He walked over and studied it closer as Cathy ducked out from the closet door.

"You and your dad? Nice picture."

Cathy's look of chagrin told him he had guessed incorrectly.

"That's me and my husband."

He swallowed and searched for something to say, but she came to his side and spoke before he could form a reply.

She picked up the photo and brushed her hand across the

glass. "Everett was thirty-eight when we married. I was nineteen."

David blinked in surprise. "Quite an age difference there." He rushed on. "But you were happy together."

She tugged at his arm. "Come on. Let's go eat and I'll tell you my love story."

He followed her into the kitchen and took a seat. She dished up two plates of spaghetti and set them on the table.

"Mind if I say grace?"

"Of course not."

They bowed their heads.

Her voice wavered. "Father, thank you for this food. Thank you for this time of companionship with David. Amen."

He opened his eyes. Her hand trembled a bit. Had he offended her and made her uncomfortable?

She gave him an odd look as he picked up his knife and fork. "Please tell me you twirl your spaghetti."

"What?" His eyebrows shot up.

"That's what the big spoon is for. Like this." She snagged some pasta onto her fork, then placed it inside the spoon and wound the spaghetti strands around the fork. "It's the only real way to eat spaghetti." She teased him with a smile. "How does an Italian food lover not know this?"

He laughed and mimicked her actions. "Not near as messy. This sauce is amazing. It has a secret ingredient."

"You'll notice it's a lot thicker than most sauces. I add chile and call it Mexican spaghetti." She shrugged. "Just a little variation I thought I'd try one day. I've been making it that way ever since."

"It's wonderful."

"Help yourself to garlic bread." She pushed the basket of bread toward him.

He took a slice and gave her a mocking look. "Already buttered. So why did you give me a knife if I wasn't supposed to cut spaghetti with it?" He wiggled his eyebrows.

She shrugged. "A place setting without a knife, fork, and spoon is incomplete. Bothers me like wearing one shoe or something. Oh!" She jumped up. "I forgot the salad." She retrieved the prepared salad from the refrigerator, placed it in the center of the table, and brought two bowls from the cabinet. "If you want to use a knife, cut up the lettuce." She grinned.

"Funny."

They ate in companionable silence for a few minutes.

She set her utensils down, wiped her mouth with her napkin, and leaned back in her chair.

"Good?" she asked.

"Better than good. It was scrumptious. I haven't eaten a meal like that in quite a while."

"I'm glad you liked it. I was afraid you'd be expecting meat and potatoes."

"Meat and potatoes are fine, but nothing beats an Italian meal for me." He patted his stomach. "I'm plenty full." He peered into the living room. "I'm surprised Horace hasn't moved the whole time we've been eating."

Cathy shook her head. "He knows very well what time he eats and he doesn't beg for table scraps."

"You've trained him well."

"I had to. He's my only companion. I wanted him to do what I needed him to do."

He crossed his hand over his chest. "Tough taskmaster."

"You can count on it."

He glanced toward the dog again, but his gaze landed and stayed locked on the picture of Cathy and her husband. He tried to tear his attention away before she noticed. When he turned back to look at her, she had the hint of a grin on her face.

"Would you like to hear about my May-December marriage?"

His face warmed. "Only if you want to tell me. It's not my business."

Her eyes took on a dreamy look. "The first time I saw Everett, I had gone to church with a neighbor. When he came strolling down the center aisle, cowboy boots flashing and spurs jangling, I thought he was the handsomest man I'd ever seen. I'd have sworn he walked right out of a western movie. We got better acquainted at a church picnic that summer. He answered my questions about horses and taught me how to ride. I had no doubt I was in love, and when he asked me to marry him, I said yes."

"What did your folks think of you marrying someone so much older than you?"

"My mom died when I was thirteen. Daddy drove a propane truck, so he was gone a lot. Neighbors watched over me more than anything, so my getting married was a load off my father's mind. Not that he had any cause for concern. He could tell that Everett loved me. Daddy knew he'd treat me well."

"And did he?"

She remained silent for a long moment. Finally, she met his eyes. "It was a hard marriage. He was a strong man, a driven man, living a hard life. I don't mean he was ever inconsiderate or cruel, because he was neither. Everett toughened me, strengthened my resolve, taught me how to brace against disappointment and broken dreams. He was a ranch foreman, and although the ranch wasn't ours, we were as emotionally invested in it as the owners. I guess with the lifestyle we led, there just wasn't time for the softer things."

His heart went out to her. "You should have known more gentleness." He looked away, then sought her face again with his gaze.

"How did your husband die? Was it a long illness?"

"No. He died working, just like I thought he would. He loved working with cattle and horses. He lived and breathed the life. One evening he went out to check the stock. When he wasn't home by midnight, I called Mr. Kincaid. That's who he worked for, the Kincaid ranch up the road about fifteen miles or so." She pointed out the window with her chin. "He went looking for Everett and found him parked on a cow trail. He'd died of a heart attack."

He took a deep breath. "Were you angry? At God?"

"Not so much when Everett died. But there was a time. We lost two babies Everett and I had hopes and dreams and plans for, and more love in our hearts than we could measure. Neither of them got to breathe a single breath of the air on this earth. Sure, I shouted my anger against God. I cried a barrelful of tears every night for weeks. I flailed my fists into the night sky against His injustice and his cruelty and the pain He had inflicted on my soul. I've seen my share of loss."

She gazed at him with deep intensity. "God does answer. You know how God answers me when I hurt?"

"Through His word."

"Yes, through scripture, and through nature. He sends a

gentle breeze that soughs through the trees at night and soothes my soul with its song. He draws my attention to the stars when one shines a little brighter than the others. It stands out as a special sign from Him to me, telling me that no matter what happens on this earth, He loves me. He always has and He always will. He paints a gorgeous sunset in the evening sky with designs no artist can match."

She pulled a small silver cross out from around her neck. "When I'm particularly distraught, I look at the cross. It reminds me of Jesus's sacrifice for us, that someday there will be no more tears, no more pain, no more wounds."

David remained silent. Pensive.

Cathy used the quiet moment to put away the leftovers.

When she sat back down, she resumed the conversation. "After Everett died, I isolated myself and didn't go anywhere. Since we lived twenty miles out of town, we weren't much involved in community life. We attended church every now and again, but for the most part, Everett worked on Sundays.

"It was months before I went anywhere. Marge called and invited me to Sunday services. I hadn't been for weeks. I read about a grief support group at the community center in the church bulletin. She had lost her mom and encouraged me to attend with her. We hit it off and kept up our friendship after the group stopped meeting. Marge recommended I apply for the church secretary position when it came open. Got me involved in the knitting club too."

He sat with his arms folded. "Do you think church helped you through any of your grief?"

"I think feeding the soul always helps us through tough times. We don't deny our bodies food when we're sick. Why

83

would we deprive ourselves of spiritual food when we're hurting? Church. Reading the Bible. Prayer."

"I go to church and I can't remember two days later a word that was spoken in the sermon. Maybe I'm not that connected." He released a deep sigh. "I don't know." He fisted his hands in front of him. "Is God up there somewhere? Yes. Does He care about me? I'm not so sure. Heather and I read the Bible together every evening, but I can't help but wonder how much I truly absorbed the words. Her either. I think we did it out of routine, because that's what you're supposed to do. Have I ever felt a close connection to God? Not in the way other people talk about. Maybe I'm just not good enough or I don't try hard enough."

"David." She reached for his hand. "I don't remember what I ate for breakfast yesterday morning, but whatever it was, it nourished my body at the time. Right? I think it's the same with our spirit. It needs to be fed on a regular basis or it shrivels up and dies." She released his hand.

"You may not feel Him close, but the wonder of it is that we don't have to be good enough or try hard enough. God gave us the gift of His son and the Holy Spirit without us asking for it or earning it or deserving it."

He drummed his fingers on the table. "If I go to church this Sunday, will you meet me in the parking lot?"

"Of course. It took someone reaching out for me to realize how much I'd been missing."

"Like you've done for me. When you invited me to breakfast a few days ago, I walked into the coffee shop with an acquaintance. I walked out with a friend."

CHAPTER 10

Cathy pumped six quarters into the pop machine in Hal's Auto Repair's waiting area and settled down on a plush looking couch away from the television. She scanned the back cover of the paperback she'd picked up at the grocery store yesterday afternoon. Her bookshelves at home burst at the seams with too many books, but no matter how she tried, she couldn't resist browsing the selection offered at the checkout counter every time she shopped. Today, a collection of Christmas miracle stories had caught her eye. The anthology ended up nestled in a sack with her other purchases.

The auto mechanic had given an estimated time of an hour for replacement of her truck's headlight. She pulled the tab on the top of the Pepsi can and stared at the broken piece of metal that came off in her hand.

Drat!

She doubted the receptionist with hair hanging down in front of her face would have access to a can opener. She set the pop can with its inaccessible liquid on the floor and opened the book. It wasn't long before the first story of a three-year-old needing emergency surgery on Christmas Eve during a blizzard in Minnesota captured her attention.

Cathy glanced up when she heard the outside door open. She blinked and broke into a grin. "If I didn't know better, I'd say you were following me."

A smile spread across David's face. "I happened to be out for a walk and noticed your vehicle in the lot. I figured there's only one gray Dodge Ram in town with a broken headlight and dented door from hitting a stop sign."

"Ha! Ha! Very funny. I thought they'd have started working on it by now. Good thing I brought a book with me."

"It's a beautiful day out. The temperature's warmed up to the high thirties." David nodded toward the window. "How about a walk over through the community center grounds? We could stroll along the lake."

"Sounds like a nice idea. I was reading this book, but seems no matter what type of waiting room you're in, there's always a TV playing either a world news channel or some dumb game show."

He helped her with her coat. "You need silence when you read?" His eyes held a hint of amusement.

"No. It's just that some noise is annoying. And my Pepsi is worthless." She retrieved the can and held it out for him to see.

"My, you've had a frustrating day. We'll stop by my Jeep and pick up a couple of waters."

"Sounds good. Thanks."

She ditched the pop in the trash receptacle before they entered the park.

"You didn't want to try to salvage it?"

"Nah." She waved her hand. "I can afford the buck and a half. Not worth the aggravation."

"Shouldn't you be working today? It's a week day."

"I'm part-time. I work nine to two Monday through Thursday. Our church doesn't have enough members to warrant a full-time secretary. We couldn't afford one either."

Cathy paced beside David in comfortable silence until they were well inside the community center property. They followed the path to the lake and skirted the shoreline.

"The ice is so thick you could drive your truck across it." David picked up a stone, pitched it, and watched it skitter across the frozen surface.

"I wouldn't want to try it. Take a mighty big fishing pole to get it out of there if you were wrong." Cathy found a smaller stone and threw it underhand like a bowling ball. It sailed through the air, bounced once, and landed a fair distance past his.

"Show off. Come on." He guided Cathy by her elbow to the gazebo. Taking a seat on the picnic table, he planted his feet on the bench. "This is my favorite spot." He splayed his arms out in front of him. "There's a break in the trees that allows the most beautiful view of the lake and the mountains. Sometimes I come here at sunrise. The colors on the frozen lake and across the snow are amazing."

"God's handiwork in all its glory. I gaze at these mountains and it brings to mind the scene from *The Sound of Music* when the Reverend Mother quotes Psalm 121. She doesn't finish it, though. Our help doesn't come from the hills. It comes from the Lord."

David shifted position and looked across the lake then turned back to her. "Great movie."

They sat quietly for a few moments. "This book I bought

today, the one I was reading at the repair shop, is about miracles God has performed at Christmas time. True stories."

His face contorted. "How does a person qualify to get one of those miracles, I wonder."

Cathy flinched. She wished she could somehow tear his pain out of him and hurl it away, but that was impossible. He would have to work through it.

"I wish I had an answer for you, David, but I don't. Jesus told us in the Bible we will face trouble in this world, but our hope is in Him."

"That's not always comforting. I guess as a person of faith it should be, but it rings hollow to me sometimes."

Cathy searched for the right words. "I think we look for the big moments, the mountaintop experiences, the magnificent miracles, and we fail to appreciate the little blessings that enrich our lives every day. I don't sense God's presence much of the time either, but every once in a while, some little thing happens and I just know His hand is in it."

She waited a long moment before she spoke again. "You're still hurting. It takes time."

"Maybe I've taken too much time." David turned toward the community center with its rustic log cabin appearance. "Shall we go inside and see what I can find to keep this feeble brain occupied? I'll pass on the knitting."

She grinned. "Ha! You're the smartest feeble-minded Scrabble player I ever met."

DAVID HAD NOT MET THE COMMUNITY CENTER DIRECTOR.

A dark-skinned man in a rolling chair sat behind an oak

desk, its edges garnished with red garland. He beckoned them in with a welcoming wave of his right hand.

Cathy nudged David forward ahead of her. "Santa, meet David Martin. David, our director, Noel Jones, commonly known as Santa around here."

The stout man, dressed in the red suit of the North Pole celebrity himself, stood and extended a firm handshake. "Welcome. Pleased to meet you." A smile, framed by his white moustache and long white beard, brightened his face. His protruding belly and dark eyes qualified him as deserving of the name as any metropolitan mall St. Nick.

"Good to meet you. I use the exercise room in the morning, but it's usually quite early."

Noel's office reflected everything Christmas. A ceramic Santa's sleigh and reindeer with Rudolph leading the pack sat on a sprawling bookshelf. A nativity set perched on Noel's desk, complete with replica shepherds, animals, and angels surrounding the baby Jesus on a bed of hay. In one corner, an assortment of candy canes, chocolate Santas, and hard candies hung from the branches of an artificial Christmas tree along with a variety of ornaments in different shapes, sizes, and colors.

"Have a candy cane?" Noel sat and waved at a display of the sweets dangling from the ceiling.

David selected a red and white candy cane and shoved it into his jacket pocket. "I'll save this for later."

Cathy plucked a multi-colored candy cane from its string and fiddled with the tight wrapper. "Santa, David wanted to check out the activities schedule. Do you have any more copies of the brochure?"

"Absolutely." He separated one from a stack on the side of

his desk and handed it to David. "Feel free to take that with you."

"I don't quite know what I'm looking for, but I'm sure I'll find something of interest."

"Do you have hobbies?" Santa asked.

"I'm handy with most tools. I'm no tradesman by any means," David shrugged, "but I'm willing to lend a hand when people need help."

Santa smiled. "Many of our seniors would benefit from your knowledge. I could put up a sign with your number."

A tap sounded on the door and Esther entered with a sheet of paper in hand.

"Hello, Cathy. David." Esther flashed a grin around the room.

A curly-haired dog David hadn't noticed, lying under Noel's desk, lifted his head and growled.

"Jolly, stop!" Noel chastised the dog.

"He's jealous. He smells my dog Smokey's scent on me." Esther ran her fingers through Jolly's white fur and scratched behind his ears. "It's okay, boy. I love you too."

The dog, content with her show of affection, lay back down and settled his head on his front paws.

David looked over the brochure and thought about Noel's question.

"Santa, I came in to remind you of your meeting with the city council tomorrow morning at nine." Esther laid the paper on his desk. "Here's your report."

"Thank you."

Esther tapped David's shoulder. "Glad to see you feeling better." She winked and exited the room.

Noel swiveled his chair back toward David. "See anything that interests you around the center itself?"

"I'm a retired math teacher. Younger grades. If you hear of any students I can help, I'd like that."

"Fine. I'll let you know."

Cathy gave David a tour of the center and introduced him to people she knew. He was acquainted with some and engaged in small talk. A group of children entered the front door amid laughter and playful shouts as they made their way down the hall and into the side rooms. A couple of them recognized David and called out greetings.

"You probably guessed that's the after-school program children," Cathy explained. "They have arts and crafts, tutoring, games."

When they got outside, he reached in his pocket and pulled out his candy cane. He loosened the wrapping, broke off a piece of candy, and popped it into his mouth.

"Do you and Heather have children?"

"One daughter." He crunched on his candy. "She and I haven't been on speaking terms since Heather died."

"I'm sorry. I can't relate to parenthood, but that must be hard."

"She blames me for her mother's death. She believes if we hadn't moved out of Denver, Heather would have been diagnosed sooner." He broke off another piece of candy. "Maybe she's right."

"It's natural to blame God or blame others when things go wrong. What about the choices we make, though? Did it occur to you that maybe Heather knew something was wrong and didn't say anything because she was scared?"

"I don't know. I suppose I never will."

The snow crunched under their feet as they crossed the lawn. When they reached the repair shop, David waited for her outside and walked her to her truck. "Thank you for spending time with me today. You could have left me to visit the center on my own. It was kind of you to introduce me and help me feel included."

"You are definitely included, David. You're a part of this community. The kids like you, and usually if you're a hit with the students, you will be with the parents too. You'll fit right in."

Was she right?

CHAPTER 11

Cathy locked up her church office for the day and tapped on Pastor Hewitt's door.

"Come on in," he called.

She inched the door open and peeked her head in. "Just wanted to let you know I'm leaving for the day."

He crooked a finger and beckoned her inside. "Sit down. We haven't had a chance to catch up for a few days. I know we've both been busy with Christmas right around the corner."

Cathy took a seat. "It crept up so fast. Seems one moment it was mid-September and the next thing you know we're planning the Christmas Eve service."

"Speaking of services—" Pastor Hewitt leaned back and hooked his hands behind his head, "—it was nice to see David Martin in church on Sunday."

"Wasn't it, though? I was so happy when he asked me if I'd meet him here. I think he felt a little awkward about the idea of walking in alone after all this time." Cathy gave the pastor a brief summary of all that transpired at Scrabble Club. "Maybe meeting someone who didn't know anything about our faith helped him realize how important it is to him. He's also signed up to tutor at the community center."

"That's great news. See how reaching out made a difference? You're good at that. Our church is blessed to have you."

Cathy's cheeks heated. "Thank you. I was disappointed Donna and Dennis didn't come to church, though. I thought they might."

"Give it time. It sounds like they've barely been introduced to the idea of God. Keep encouraging them. You say you gave them a Bible?"

"I gave one to Donna when I saw her at knitting group at the community center."

"Good." Pastor Hewitt motioned toward the bookshelf towering above him on the wall. "I have extra copies here if you run across someone else who needs one."

"I'll keep that in mind." She steepled her hands under her chin. "Ever since we talked to the Walkers, I hear Maybelle Lovejoy's voice in the back of my head. She was so intense with her message the day I met her. It was as though she was recruiting me to a mission. Now I feel this drive to fulfill that mission."

"You will. Just don't try to get ahead of God." He chuckled. "We tend to do that. We go running off trying to find our own direction when maybe He has a reason for not showing it to us quite yet. He'll put the people in your path he wants you to reach."

A woman shuffled down the sidewalk as Cathy walked across the church parking lot. She wore a pair of ordinary house shoes and her coat hung open. A plastic sack dangled from her wrist.

Cathy would recognize those thin tufts of gray hair anywhere. Nellie Crabtree. Should she offer the old woman a ride? By the time Cathy warmed up her car and got out to the street, Nellie was a mere half a block from her house. No point in chasing her down now.

A notion entered her head, so far-fetched and yet so strong that she had to follow it through. She parked at the grocery store and stopped at the checkout counter. Thank God her friend Wendy from the knitting club was working. She waited until Wendy finished checking her last customer before she approached.

Wendy greeted Cathy with a smile. "Hey, girl, that sweater you're working on is really coming along. You're going like a snowball rolling down a hill on that thing."

Cathy grinned. "Yeah, thanks. Have you noticed Nellie Crabtree in here in the last little while?"

Wendy's face fell. "She was here a few minutes ago. Maybe a half hour. Bought a box of crackers and a can of cat food. Poor old thing. I swear I think she lives on crackers and water. Her daughter used to check on her, but I haven't seen her for several days."

"Thanks, Wendy."

OK, Lord, Cathy prayed when she returned to her car. *You put this in my lap. Now equip me to handle it. And please encourage David to say yes when I ask for his help.*

Three fifteen. The food bank didn't close until four o'clock. She ran by the community center and parked at the gym back entrance. A young girl Cathy didn't recognize sat at the desk. "Have you been here before?" she asked.

Cathy shook her head. "No, I haven't."

"OK. Just fill out this simple form for our records." She

flashed Cathy an encouraging smile and waved. "The signs tell you how much of each item you can take."

"Thank you so much." Cathy filled two grocery sacks with canned goods, bread, milk, eggs, fresh fruit, and vegetables. She stopped by the church, accessed the back door, and picked up a three-foot tall artificial Christmas tree, two boxes of ornaments, a string of lights, and some tinsel, all from the 'give away' box.

She went home and put the perishable groceries away. Should she call David or text? She decided on a text. Less intrusive in case he didn't want to answer.

HI, DAVID. ARE YOU BUSY TOMORROW?

She waited for a reply. Her palms moistened. That was stupid. She didn't know if he even owned a cell phone or if she had texted a land line.

The reply came back a moment later.

WHO IS THIS?

SO SORRY. THIS IS CATHY.

Her phone rang. Cathy's mouth went dry. She took a deep breath and swiped the screen. "Hi, David. I didn't mean to bother you, but I—"

"I didn't recognize the number. You've only talked to me on the church phone. I'm terrible at texting, so decided to just call. What's going on tomorrow? And since when are you bothering me?"

Her heart lurched a bit at his welcoming tone. "I have a plan. I need your help."

"I told Dennis Walker I'd stop by his place and evaluate some work he needs done on his house. It's his day off, so I can go over there any time. Then I'll be tutoring the Johnson kids at four. What's the plan?"

Lord, I like this man.

"It could be dangerous."

"Sounds intriguing. A plan for what?" She could hear the amusement in his voice.

She rushed on before she lost her nerve. "To spread Christmas joy. We might get attacked instead."

He chuckled. "That does sound interesting. Are we going to play Robin Hood? Steal from the rich and give to the poor?"

She could visualize his raised eyebrows. "Not quite. Can you meet me at the corner where I had my accident? Eleven o'clock."

"I'll be there."

DAVID WHISTLED THE OPENING BARS TO *HARK! THE HERALD Angels Sing* as he parked his car on the corner where he had stopped to help Cathy a mere few days ago. A lot had happened in that short span of time.

Cathy had broken the ice with her plea for help with the church decorating and cracked his shell during their conversation at breakfast. Her compassionate attitude toward his grief, especially after he had learned about her own, had prompted him to take a good look at himself. He had been simply existing, going through the day-to-day motions of functioning with no purpose.

His return to church last Sunday had not healed his hurting heart, but it had acted as a soothing balm to ease the pain a bit. Cathy had ignited a spark that inspired him to feed his soul again. He even sensed God's presence for the first time in a long while. Just this morning, he had opened his Bible and read a few passages of scripture.

Life would never be the same without Heather, but perhaps new challenges awaited. His meeting with Cathy this morning might prove to be an adventure.

She pulled up and hopped out of her truck.

David stepped out of his vehicle. "Here we are. What's next?"

"Are you ready to do battle?" She pointed with a jut of her chin.

David glanced in the direction she indicated. Nellie Crabtree's house. "You're kidding."

She put her hand on his arm. "I have peace offerings." Her expression turned serious. "That lady needs help, David. I don't know if she'll accept it or not, but we've got to try. I brought food from the food bank and Christmas decorations from the church giveaway box. I thought we could spruce up the inside with some Christmas spirit."

David studied her for a long moment. "Let's start unloading."

He pulled the box of decorations from the back of the truck, and she looped the sacks of food over her arm.

She clutched his hands and bowed her head. *"Dear God, please be with us."*

The two trod up the sidewalk. Cathy stopped in front of the

doorbell and poised her finger over it. "Here goes." She took a deep breath and pushed the button.

No response.

They waited a full minute before he said, "Try again."

A few heartbeats later, they heard approaching footsteps.

Slow.

Shuffling.

The door creaked open and Nellie stood before them in a pair of black slacks and a long white woolen sweater, high top shoes on her feet. She scrutinized the two of them, then swung the door wider. "May I help you?"

"Nellie, I'm David." He swallowed. "This is Cathy. We brought you some things we thought you would like for Christmas."

Nellie patted her forehead. "Yes. Cathy and David." She smiled.

Cathy looked to David.

He nodded.

"May we come in?"

"Yes, of course. Christmas did you say? It's Christmastime already." She stepped aside for the two to enter.

The first thing David noticed in the small living room was the extraordinary number of religious items that decorated the walls. Large and small plaques showed the Lord's Prayer, others various Bible verses. A picture of Jesus hung in the center of one wall and a silver cross adorned another. A blanket thrown over the couch depicted Genesis 1:1 against a backdrop of a starry sky with the earth in the background. Nellie stood right behind him. He turned to speak. "You have a lot of nice things."

Nellie patted her hair, then inched close to David and stared. "Who did you say you are?"

"I'm David." He pointed toward the kitchen. "Cathy and I brought you some food."

Cathy had stepped into the kitchen and put the sacks on the table.

Nellie shuffled over. "Food." She opened the refrigerator door. "Milk goes right here. I see you brought milk."

"Yes," Cathy answered, "and eggs. Fruit. Vegetables." Cathy placed the items on the near empty shelves. A couple of containers with some kind of leftovers, an apple, a tub of butter, and a jar of strawberry jam. An open box of baking soda sat on the top shelf.

"Where would you like me to put these? We have bread, soup, canned meat, beef stew. Cereal for breakfast."

"What a delightful surprise." Nellie opened a cabinet door to reveal three boxes of saltine crackers. She sank into a cushioned kitchen chair. "Won't you sit down? I can fix you lunch." She folded her hands in front of her. "We always thank Jesus for our food first."

Cathy glanced at David. "We're not really hungry. We brought you a Christmas tree. Would you like us to decorate it for you?"

Nellie clapped her hands. "Oh, how lovely!"

David and Cathy retrieved the artificial tree and box of decorations. They made short work of setting the tree in a corner and trimming it. Nellie watched in wonderment, offering an occasional comment. "I think this ornament would look lovely right there." She would wave her hand at a branch and David would move the ornament accordingly. They omitted lights, fearing Nellie could trip over the cord in an

CATHY'S CHRISTMAS CONFESSION

attempt to unplug them. The little tree with its red balls and silver tinsel brightened up the room.

Nellie sat on the couch and admired the tree, then lifted her eyes to the cross on the opposite wall. "It's Jesus's birthday." She reached a bony hand out to David. "Did you know that?"

David sat beside her and patted her hand. "I do know that."

She peered deep into David's eyes. "Jesus loves you. He loves you."

Cathy took a seat on the other side of Nellie. "Jesus loves you too, and He knows we are worried about you. Can you tell us if anyone comes by to take care of you, maybe to do some cleaning in your house and prepare your food?"

She patted Cathy's cheek. "Yes, Mrs. Farmer takes good care of me. I like Mrs. Farmer, but she doesn't like my cat. I have to lock him away when Mrs. Farmer is here." Her face crumpled. "I think my Mittens is sick." She searched David's face. "Would you look at Mittens for me?"

David gave Cathy a what do I say look.

"Sure." Cathy nodded. "We'd like to meet Mittens."

The old woman stood and made her way down the hall.

David shot Cathy a pained look. He knew nothing about animals.

When Nellie returned, she cradled a towel in her arms. She unfolded the towel and stroked the gray fluffy fur with long, loving strokes. She handed the towel wrapped Mittens to David.

Fake fur.

Stained white feet.

He swallowed hard.

"Nellie—I—I think Mittens needs some water. Let me give him a drink."

101

David turned on a thin stream of water at the kitchen sink and cleaned the toy as best he could. He wrapped it in the towel and handed it to Nellie. "If you keep Mittens warm for the rest of the day, I think he'll be fine."

Nellie's face broke out in a bright smile. "He looks better already. Thank you. I think I must rest now." She moved to her rocking chair with Mittens tight against her chest. "Thank you for making my Mittens better. I was worried."

"We'll be going now, Nellie." David started toward the door, but Cathy motioned for him to wait.

"One last thing. Nellie, do you have a daughter?"

Nellie's face brightened. "Yes, my daughter Hannah. We talk on the telephone. Her telephone number is on my refrigerator."

"That's wonderful. You have a good day."

Cathy eased over to the refrigerator, then David and Cathy slipped quietly out the door. When they arrived at her truck, Cathy leaned against the door and sobbed. David cradled her close and rocked her gently in his embrace. "Oh, David. A stuffed animal." She wiped tears away with her glove. "How very sad."

"I know." He patted Cathy's back. "You are a remarkable lady and you did an amazing thing for that woman in there today."

"I was nervous. I didn't know how she would react after the way she carried on the day of the accident. I don't think she even knew I'm the same person."

"She probably didn't."

"I'm going to call her daughter. I memorized the number. It's in this area code, so she can't live too far away."

Cathy called from her cell phone, but no one answered and there was no option to leave a message.

"I'll try again this evening. Maybe she works. In the meantime, I'm starving and I want an egg salad sandwich."

David frowned. "I don't know of any place in town that serves them."

"You're right, but I have two in a cooler in my car. After you agreed to this venture with me, the least I can do is feed you lunch."

He cocked an eyebrow. "This is the third time the same woman has invited me out to eat. I'm going to get a reputation."

She laughed. "Come on. Get in your car and follow me. We'll eat in the gazebo at the community center."

"Why not? We're having a heat wave. It's got to be at least forty."

CHAPTER 12

Cathy buzzed Hannah's number and prayed for someone to answer. "Hello?"

"Hello, Hannah?" Her mouth went dry. What would this woman think of a total stranger going into her mother's house?

"Yes, this is Hannah. May I help you?"

"Hi, my name is Cathy Fischer and I'm calling about your mom." Her words rushed out in a torrent as she told the story of her and David's visit to Nellie's home.

"Oh, my goodness, Mrs. Fischer. I'm so glad you called. I'd been visiting Mama when I could and I call her every few days. She sounded so good. No food in the house you say?"

"There wasn't much. A couple of containers of leftovers in the refrigerator, soup maybe. Crackers in the cabinet."

"Mama loves her crackers. She was getting deliveries from the market. Don't they do delivery service anymore?"

"I can't say. I hope you don't mind that we—a friend and I—brought her food we thought she could use. We put some decorations up for Christmas for her too. We didn't know if she had anyone to look after her or—"

"I've not been able to come visit for a month. I fell on the ice and broke my ankle, haven't been able to drive. Maybe I better get someone to give me a ride up there so I can find out what's going on." Her voice turned hard. "Mrs. Farmer cleans her house. She should have told me what was going on. I'm sorry you had to be inconvenienced."

"It was no inconvenience. In fact, it was a blessing to be able to share some Christmas joy."

"I thank you so very much. I'll do my best to get there in the next couple of days."

"That would be wonderful. I have one other question for you. Did you know your mom seems very attached to a stuffed animal. She thinks it's real."

Hannah chuckled. "Yes, I know all about Mittens. My Daddy gave her that toy when they were dating. She's kept it all these years. She's developed the delusion that he's real. It's part of her mental illness, but harmless."

Cathy breathed a sigh of relief. "I'm glad you told me. If there's anything I can do, please let me know. Oh, and Hannah. Happy Jesus's birthday!"

CATHY PRINTED OFF A COPY OF THE SUNDAY BULLETIN AND placed it in the copy machine. After she had run the front side, she positioned the finished copies in the tray and set the machine to run the inside page. She heard the front door open and stepped out of the office to see who had entered.

"David. Come on in. Coffee?"

"No thanks. I was driving by and thought I'd stop to tell you my news." He pulled up a folding chair and sat.

"I hope it's good news. Should I be sitting down for it too?" She laughed as she turned to retrieve the bulletins.

"Santa Noel is going to initiate my handyman program at the community center."

Just as he spoke, Cathy took the sheets of paper from the tray and laid them on the table. "Oh no!" She slapped her forehead.

David looked at her in confusion. "What? I thought you'd be happy."

"No, not that. Of course, I'm happy for you. Look what I did."

"What?"

"I printed the inside of these bulletins upside down. All fifty of them." She stared at the offending pages with hands on her hips.

"I'm sorry." David clasped his hands together in front of him. "I shouldn't have distracted you. It's probably my fault."

"No, it's all mine. I set the machine to run before you got here. It's not that big a deal, but it bothers me to waste all this paper." She dropped into her desk chair, propped her elbow against its arm and rested her forehead in her palm. "I hate it when I'm so darned absent-minded."

"You're being awful tough on yourself. It was an honest mistake."

"I suppose. So, tell me about your new program."

"It's nothing fancy, just teaching people the basics of how to hammer a nail, use a screwdriver, a wrench. Things like that. It may sound crazy, but there's a lot of people out there who don't know any of that."

Cathy smiled. "It doesn't sound crazy. I don't know the first thing about tools or how to use them. I'd benefit from a class like that. Look at you go. I'm so proud of you. I knew you'd accomplish great things once you found something you like to do."

"I owe you a big thank you. If it weren't for you encouraging me, I'd still be sitting at home doing nothing."

"We all need a little help now and again."

David's eyes brightened. "I have other news. I don't know if you're aware, but the center is doing a baking contest. I entered us in it."

Cathy gaped at him. "You what?"

"Contestants can be single or in teams of two, so I signed us up. I know how much you love to bake cookies and how good they are. We could have a lot of fun with it." He hurried on. "I hope it's okay, but I don't have an oven in my apartment, so we'd have to do the baking in your kitchen."

Cathy tried to conjure up an enthusiastic reply. Instead, she looked away and toyed with her necklace. How could she tell hm this was a horrible idea? She couldn't do that, not after he had immersed himself into the life of the community center with such eagerness, and at her prompting. She managed to produce a weak smile. "That would be fine."

"Here's the details." He took a piece of paper from his pocket and handed it to her.

She studied the cheerful flyer with a border of Christmas trees along the sides. A speech balloon came from the mouth of a big Santa at the top of the page that proclaimed the Christmas Ridge Community Center Baking Contest. Pictures of cakes and cookies decorated the sheet and a set off square was marked Rules.

- Amateur contestants only
- Item cannot be purchased (must be baked)
- Decorate with traditional Christmas colors
- Categories: 8u, 9-13, 14-18, adult
- Items judged based on decorative appearance
- Entry form due by December 15th by 4:00 p.m.
- Entries due Dec 21st at 4:00 p.m.
- Items will be auctioned
- Proceeds to benefit CRCC

"A baking and fundraiser combination. The age group division is a good idea. Makes it fairer that way." She started to hand the flyer back.

David waved it away. "Keep it. I have another."

"I suppose we can do this." She tried to inject eagerness into her voice, but the words came out forced. Had David noticed?

"Should we bake that day?"

"Why don't you plan to come out to the house on Saturday. We can freeze whatever we make."

That would give her time to seek advice on something she knew nothing about.

CATHY PALMED HER CELL PHONE AND DIALED HER NIECE Krystin in Nashville.

"Aunt Cathy! How are you?" Krystin's spirited voice always chirped with the excitement of a child on Christmas morning. "Thank you for the cookie orders you've placed. My goodness, I never expected you would need so many. What are you doing, feeding them to the mountain goats?"

Cathy chuckled. "No, sweet girl, but I have a lot of hungry people here in town who love them. I bring them to events at church, at our community center, and I donate some to the food bank. We have several events going on at this time of year."

"I know. Business is picking up because of the approaching holiday. I'm thrilled the bakery is doing so well."

"That's great news." Cathy's voice flattened. "Krystin, I need your help."

"Sure. Anything. What's wrong?"

"What's wrong is that I haven't been honest with my friends in Christmas Ridge and it's gotten me into trouble. I'm embarrassed to admit it, but I never told them I buy the cookies. My friend David thinks I—"

Krystin interrupted. "Your friend David? Are you dating someone, Auntie? And you didn't tell me?"

"No, no. It's nothing like that."

Is it?

Surely, she and David weren't dating.

Or were they?

A moment of confusion attacked her brain. "Wait a minute. Let's start again." She tapped her fingers on the arm of her chair. "David is a friend who lost his wife and this is his first Christmas alone. I'm helping him get through the Christmas season. I got him involved in the community center and he signed us up for a baking contest and—" She paused and took a deep breath. "Sweetie, he doesn't know I can't bake."

"Relax." Krystin chuckled. "Anyone can bake."

CATHY'S CHRISTMAS CONFESSION

"Maybe so, but not like you can. He thinks I've baked all those amazing cookies you've sent."

"Before you get too panicked, do you know what the rules are? How sophisticated are we talking?"

"Hold on." What had she done with that flyer David gave her? After a frantic search, she found it rumpled in a jacket pocket. She smoothed it out and read the rules out loud.

"Okay, so you're not exactly competing with Pillsbury here." Cathy could hear Krystin's grin in her voice. "I think you can get through this unscathed. First of all, taste is not the main issue. Of course, you want whatever you bake to taste good to whoever ends up eating it, but you don't have to worry about being competitive in that area."

"Right."

"I would recommend you go with a basic sugar cookie recipe, buy canned frosting, food coloring, red and green sprinkles, and Christmas cookie cutters. You do have everything else you need for baking, right?"

"Um." Cathy hesitated. "Dare I ask what else I need?"

"Well, for one, a couple of cookie sheets are essential."

"Oh yeah, huh. Nope, don't have any."

"A rolling pin. Pastry mat. Measuring cups and spoons. A cooling rack. Non-stick cooking spray. A flour sifter would come in handy. You have an electric mixer, don't you? And maybe a mixing bowl or two?"

"I do make mashed potatoes on occasion." Cathy released a nervous laugh. "And I'm supposed to know what to do with all this other stuff?"

"Don't worry. I'll email you a couple of simple recipes with detailed instructions."

Cathy sighed. "Thanks, sweetie. I'm counting on you."

"You do know how to use the oven." A hint of doubt crept into Krystin's voice. "Right?"

"Of course."

She had heated garlic bread in the thing. Surely, she could bake cookies. Right?

CHAPTER 13

David knocked at Cathy's front door and she beckoned him inside. Like his first visit, she greeted him with a tail wagging Horace next to her minus the ferocious barking welcome. Recalling the routine from last time, David extended his hand to connect with the dog's outstretched paw. "That's amazing." He chuckled as Horace dipped his head and licked David's hand in greeting.

"He knows you now." Cathy patted the dog's head. "He's a friendly boy, but he can look and act threatening when I need him to."

"Glad you have adequate protection." He slipped off his jacket.

"Let me hang that in here." She hung up his jacket and waved him to follow her. "I've been fortunate not to have any kind of trouble out here, not the bad kind anyway. An occasional stray cow or horse wanders through the yard every now and again and I have to alert the sheriff, but no human strangers."

"You've put up a tree and garland and all kinds of stuff

since I was last here." He walked over and studied a ceramic Christmas village. "Very nice."

"I have Marge to thank for this. She goes all out with decorating. You think this looks good. You should see her house. Come on out to the kitchen."

He exaggerated a deep sniff. "Hmm, I detect the lingering aroma of spaghetti sauce."

She grinned. "That wouldn't be a hint for an invite to another Italian meal, would it?"

"What would ever make you think such a thing?" He took a seat at the table. "I appreciated your hospitality and that big container of leftover sauce you gave me. I froze some for another day."

"I was glad to do it. Would you like a water or anything to drink?"

"No. I'm fine, thanks." He settled back in the upholstered kitchen chair and slung his arm over its back. He watched Cathy as she opened a cabinet door and pulled down two mixing bowls and a set of measuring cups.

She turned and narrowed her eyes. "Don't get too comfortable. You're going to work, mister."

"You just say the word, boss. Tell me what to do."

She jutted her chin toward a grocery tote at the end of the counter. "There's new sacks of flour and sugar in there. Open them and pour them in these." She motioned toward a set of four white ceramic canisters.

He opened the bag of flour and prepared to dump it.

"Gently," Cathy warned. "Pour it gently. We don't want flour dust all over everything."

When he had filled the canisters, he turned to see her studying a recipe card. He peered over her shoulder. "World's

114

Best Sugar Cookies," he read. "And who determined they're the best in the world?"

"The person who wrote it, I guess." She chuckled. "So, the first thing we want to do is measure out three cups of flour."

"I can do that."

He measured the flour and dumped it into the small bowl while Cathy prepared a mixture of butter and sugar in the larger one. He picked up the recipe. "Baking powder?"

"Cabinet over the sink. Left side." She reached into a drawer and pulled out a set of measuring spoons. "Teaspoon." She separated the correct spoon from the others on a plastic ring.

"Yes, ma'am." He added the powder to the flour.

"Reach me an egg, would you?"

"Sure." He opened the refrigerator and retrieved a single egg left in the carton and set the empty carton on the table.

She turned off the mixer. "How good are you at cracking eggs?"

"I'm a cracker jack egg cracker." He grinned at his play on words.

"Yeah, well, I always use caution." She opened a cabinet door above her head and pulled out a cereal dish. "Crack it into this in case your cracking skills are not as cracker jack as you think and you get some shell in there."

"If you say so, boss."

David cupped the egg in his palm and whacked it against the rim of the dish the way he had seen Heather do it. The dish sailed off the counter and clattered to the floor.

Cathy leaned against the counter, covered her face with her hands, and burst out laughing.

115

He looked from her to the uncooperative egg and back to her again. "What's going on?"

"I— That egg. That egg is—" Another peal of laughter interrupted her words.

He joined in with a chuckle, although he wasn't sure what was so funny.

"It's—It's hard-boiled!"

A noise drew David's attention. A mass of black and white fur hurtled headlong into the kitchen. "Look out!" he shouted.

"No, Horace! Down, boy!" Cathy's frantic commands went unheeded.

Horace raced across the kitchen tile, swiped a giant paw along the counter, and hooked the plastic bowl of flour. It rolled on its side, then toppled to the floor and landed upside down in a heap of white powder.

Cathy scolded the dog, who lay down in the middle of the floor as though his behavior was nothing unusual. "Out, Horace! Get out!" She opened the front door. He gave her a forlorn look, then meandered out into the yard.

"I don't know what possessed him to do that." She stared at the mess as though it would clean itself if they waited long enough.

David sighed. "At least the bowl was plastic. That's something to be thankful for."

She scooped as much as she could into the bowl and dumped it in the trash.

"Cathy." He brushed flour dust off his shoes. "How do we begin to clean the rest of this up?"

"Definitely not with water." She put one hand on her hip and braced herself against the counter. "Let me think. A vacuum cleaner is out. The fine dust would clog up the motor

116

CATHY'S CHRISTMAS CONFESSION

something terrible. I guess we could start with a broom and dust pan." She reached into a utility closet

"Makes sense."

"I'll tell you one thing." Cathy swiped her forehead with her forearm after the fifth trip to the trash can. "Three cups of flour looks like a lot more spilled than it does in a bowl."

"That's for sure." David scraped flour off the counter into a dish with a knife. They soaked up the rest with wet paper towels.

Cathy took the incident in stride, making light of the situation as though it were a simple water spill on the counter.

Heather would not have been so calm. She would have ranted over the mess for days.

Once the flour was cleaned and the counter wiped, they began the process over again, this time hoping for a better outcome.

"How was it for you to be back in church last Sunday?" Cathy pressed a Christmas tree cookie cutter into the soft dough.

"It was—it was good." He formed a reindeer and placed it on the cookie sheet. "I appreciate you meeting me. I expected to feel like a stranger, but folks who know me made me feel welcome. Pastor Hewitt and I chatted in his office after the service."

"I'm flattered you asked me to go with you."

"Of course, I would ask you." He paused with the bell-shaped cookie cutter in his hand. "I don't think you realize how much support you are for me. You make me smile. You make me laugh. Most of all, you bring relief to my bruised soul. I probably wouldn't have gone back to church at all if it wasn't for you."

117

He set the cookie cutter down and watched her fill the last space on the cookie sheet.

She looked up and met his gaze.

"You are a special friend." His voice wavered. "More than a special friend."

The words hung in the air. When had his heart strayed over that line?

She picked up the sheet of cookies and slid it into the oven.

When she sat again, she reached across the table and squeezed his hand. "You're special to me as well. I enjoy every moment we spend together. But I don't want to push you into something you're not ready for."

He squeezed back, then relinquished his hold and folded his hands on the table. "It's only fair to tell you, I bring issues to a relationship."

She shrugged. "We all do to one degree or another."

"No one in Christmas Ridge knows, but I grew up in foster care." He folded his arms in front of him and leaned on the table. "My parents were not—adequate parents. I was removed from our home when I was two. My older brother was five. We were bounced around from family to family when we were young. Finally, we both ended up in a stable home together, but I developed a fear of being separated from the people I love."

"David, I'm so sorry." Her eyes shone with sympathy.

"It was difficult when my brother aged out of the system, went off to college. I was barely a freshman and felt abandoned again. I was fortunate to spend my high school years in a caring home with good foster parents, but I was an angry, lonely young man. I took my anger out on everyone around me, especially Frank and Nancy Martin." He shook his

118

CATHY'S CHRISTMAS CONFESSION

head and fisted his hands together under his chin. "They worked with me, loved me, even adopted me. They introduced me to the church, to Jesus. Looking back, I realize now it was God who brought them into my life."

He stared past Cathy and out the window for a long moment. "When Heather died, I felt abandoned again. By her. Mostly by God. I let all that anger, and fear, and loneliness back in. I've been long on blaming God for all the pain in my life and short on thanking Him for the blessings. I don't deserve His forgiveness."

"You don't. None of us do. His forgiveness is a gift, remember? Jesus is the gift. He died for us while we were still sinners." She paused. "Did you and Heather ever get angry at each other, blame each other sometimes?"

"Of course."

"You forgave each other, didn't you?"

"But that's not the same. We're not supposed to get angry at God."

She raised her eyebrows. "Who says so? God created you. He loves you even more than she did, more than anyone ever could. God knows you're angry with Him. He knew you would get angry with Him before you even got angry with Him. Your anger is no surprise to God. He will forgive you, but you have to ask Him. You say you've turned your back on God. Turn around and you'll see God hasn't gone anywhere. He's been there all the time."

David fidgeted with a cookie cutter. "I hope you're right."

The oven timer dinged and Cathy pulled the cookies out. She frowned. "These do not look right." She checked the oven, then swiped the recipe off the table. "Oh no!"

"What?"

119

"I set the temperature at fifty degrees less than it should be. Huge mistake. I don't know if we can even salvage these." She cranked the temperature up. "Why am I always so stupid?" She sat and clenched her fists.

"Stop it, Cathy. Stop beating yourself up." He came around the table. "Look at me."

She met his gaze.

He brushed a tear from her cheek. Her skin felt smooth under his touch. "Let's take a break, go sit in your living room by the fire for a few minutes and relax. It's been a bit of a stressful day."

She offered a weak smile. "OK. I can fix coffee."

"Show me where it is and I'll fix the coffee. You go spend time with Horace. I'm sure he's feeling neglected."

"Thank you. Coffee is in the small canister and Horace knows he's in the doghouse." She removed the cookie sheet from the oven. "Mugs are in the cabinet above the dishes."

When he arrived in the living room, he found Cathy kneeling on the floor rubbing Horace's belly. "I see you let him back in and you two have reconciled."

"He knows I can't stay mad at him for long." She took a seat on the couch.

He handed her a mug of steaming coffee. "Careful, it's hot."

She blew on it and took a sip. "You remembered the cream and sugar. Just the way I like it." She turned to him with a smile. "It's been a long time since anyone waited on me like this."

David took a seat on the opposite end of the couch. "You deserve to be waited on."

She blushed and stared into the fire.

"Do you know what impressed me most about you the day we met at the coffee shop?" He leaned in closer to Cathy.

She answered with a teasing smile. "That I take cream and sugar in my coffee?"

He chuckled, then looked away. When he met her inquisitive eyes, his throat constricted. "I—I was thankful you referred to Heather by her name rather than 'your wife.'" He swallowed. "You asked me about her like you were interested. Like you truly cared."

"I did care, David, and I was interested. When Everett died, most people acted like they thought I would dissolve into a puddle of tears if they mentioned his name. I wanted to talk about him, share stories, memories, but no one asked. People forget that even though our loved ones are gone, they're still in our hearts." She brought her palm to her chest. "They'll always be right here."

David shifted position and took a drink of coffee. "I feel a connection to someone for the first time in a long while. It means a great deal to me. You've brought me back from a very lonely place. I like it here."

TWO HOURS LATER, CATHY INSPECTED THE COLLECTION OF cookies spread out on the counter and the table. She selected the ones that looked the best and put them into a plastic container. "We have barely enough decent cookies to enter in this contest. Half of them look underbaked, the other half are burned on the bottom. Unless you want to try again tomorrow."

"These are fine by me. I don't think I could stand another round of baking." He chuckled. "This is hard work."

"I'll put these in the freezer and thaw them out the morning of the contest." She refilled her coffee mug and leaned against the counter. "You told me about turning your back on God. Now I have to make a confession. It's been bothering me for a while, but never more than today."

He furrowed his brow. "Sit down. Tell me about it."

She ran her palm along the pastry board and toyed with the small particles of excess dough. "When I became involved in the community, I had nothing to offer. No skill. No talent. The first time I was asked to volunteer, I offered to bring cookies. My niece in Nashville had just opened an online bakery. I wanted to help her out, so her business was the ideal solution." She sighed. "Over time, my reputation for these different cookies grew. I can't bake. I don't know the first thing about it." She raised her eyes to meet his. "I'm a fake. A sham. I've been hiding this secret for months now. I need to tell the truth."

"Have you told people you bake the cookies?"

She shook her head. "No. Never. That would be a blatant lie."

He frowned. "Then what are you worried about?"

"I don't like deceiving people. I should have told you the moment you mentioned the contest that I can't bake. You even believed that I love to bake. HA! What a joke." Her voice rose and she choked on her next words. "My friends have an expectation of me, and if they find out I'm not who they think I am…" Tears spilled down her cheeks.

"You think your friends will judge you based on your cookies? That's absurd." He came over and put his arm around her shoulders. "I don't care if you can bake. They probably

CATHY'S CHRISTMAS CONFESSION

don't either. That's not the most important thing about you. The most important thing is your big heart, your desire to help, to care, to reach out. That's all that matters. Don't you see?"

"You really think so?"

He squatted and cupped her cheeks in his hands. "I know so. I entered us in this contest because I thought it would be fun for the two of us. I didn't mean to upset you. We'll enter these cookies and we'll have a good time. Maybe we'll tell the story of the egg and Horace and the flour and make people laugh. That's what will count. Sharing Christmas joy." He kissed her forehead. "Isn't that what you've wanted to do?"

"Joy and Jesus. People need to know why we celebrate Christmas. I want to tell them about Jesus. I just don't know how."

"Come here." He nudged her out of her chair and wrapped his arms around her. "Just be yourself. That's how you tell everyone you meet about Jesus. Look what you did for Nellie and her daughter. Look what you did for Donna and Dennis. You walked into their lives and you planted seeds.

"Cathy, you've shown me Jesus in everything you've done since the day I found your truck buried in the snow on that street corner. I had nothing to look forward to but a Christmas full of empty loneliness. You put the meaning back in the season for me. You set me on the path back to God with your words and your actions and your kindness and the love that radiates from you for Him. I'll always be grateful."

She leaned into David's embrace and relished his comfort, his reassurance, his gentleness.

"I want to do more."

123

CHAPTER 14

When David slipped into the pew next to Cathy the following morning, she sensed something different about him. He exuded a peace she hadn't noticed before. His eyes held a gladness that made her curious to find out what had changed. He had joined her just before the service began, so she was unable to ask questions.

The music brought joy to her heart as they sang *The First Noel*, *Away in a Manger*, and *Joy to the World*.

Pastor Hewitt's sermon, titled *Who Will See Jesus in You This Christmas?* spoke right to her heart. She wanted everyone she met to see Jesus's love, but she didn't know how to accomplish that.

Lord, please show me what you want me to do. Show me how to bring the Christmas story to those who don't know it. Show me where to spread Christmas joy.

When the service ended, Wendy approached her.

"Did you hear about Nellie Crabtree?"

Cathy's heart skipped a beat. "No. Something happened to her?"

"Her daughter Hannah is here. She'll be taking her mother to live with her."

Relief washed over Cathy. "I'm so glad to hear that."

"You've entered the baking contest, haven't you? Of course, we all expect you did." Cathy thought about the collection of cookies sitting in her freezer. "Yes, David Martin and I teamed up."

"Oh good. I'm going to watch for your entry so I can bid on it."

Wendy hurried off.

A stab of guilt attacked Cathy. She didn't care what David thought, she had to admit her deception. No better place to make a Christmas confession than at the contest.

When David was ready to leave, she rushed outside with him. "Tell me, what's different?"

He wore a wide grin. "You can tell?"

"Something has changed. And I think it's a good change."

His face lit up. "I had a talk with God last night. A long, honest, heartfelt talk. I feel connected again, Cathy."

"That's wonderful. I'm so happy for you."

"I feel lighter, more at peace, like I just dropped a huge weight off my shoulders." He sobered. "Still missing Heather, of course, but with a different kind of longing. It's just a desire to hold on to her memory, but I don't feel that desperate loneliness I'd been carrying around for so long."

"Praise God. I knew He was there for you all the time. You just had to tell Him you want Him back in your life."

He smiled. "I do."

"Would you like to come out to the house? I really have to talk something over with you."

CATHY'S CHRISTMAS CONFESSION

"All right." His eyes registered concern. "Is everything okay?"

"No. Just when things are getting right for you, they're going all wrong for me."

"Let me run home and change clothes. I'll be out in a few minutes."

Cathy brewed coffee and waited for David's arrival. Would he understand how deeply she felt about her deception, or would he think her silly?

She met him at the front door without speaking. He followed her into the kitchen. Her hands trembled as she set a mug of coffee in front of him. "Sorry. I didn't even ask you if you wanted that."

He ignored the comment. "Cathy, what's wrong?"

"You know how you felt when you were—well—out of touch with God?"

He nodded.

"I don't feel out of touch, but I sense that he's trying to give me a message and I'm not hearing it. I never told you this story, but I met the most incredible lady a few weeks ago. She wished me a Happy Jesus's birthday and then she told me to share Christmas joy and introduce Jesus to others. I thought it a strange comment at the time because I assumed everyone knew about Jesus. Then I had a talk with Pastor Hewitt and he explained that so many people don't. Maybe even people in our own church.

"When I saw how sad and lonely you were, I thought I could bring you some Christmas joy and I hope I've done that. I just learned today that Nellie Crabtree is going to live with her daughter. That's good. Donna and Dennis." She shook her

127

head. "I'm disappointed they haven't accepted your invitation to come to church. I want to reach others like them. But I feel like I'm unworthy to do anything until I come clean about this baking scheme."

"Oh, for Heaven's sake. This is why you're so upset? It's hardly a scheme."

"I'm going to go to that sale Wednesday with those pathetic looking cookies we baked and people are going to know something isn't right."

His face clouded. "We can just not show up at the contest at all. If this is such a big deal, maybe we should forget the whole thing."

She pounded her fist on the table. "That won't solve anything. I wanted you to know, I'm going to that contest and I'm going to confess what I've been doing. Just like you needed to forgive God, I need to be forgiven by the people of this town. If you can't understand that, I'm sorry."

"If it's that important to you, I'll be there with you, but I doubt anyone is going to care. I don't get the connection between this confession you feel you have to make and how it's going to help spread Christmas joy or tell people about Jesus, but I'll stand by you."

"Thank you."

"I told Dennis I'd work on the project at his house today, so I guess I'll see you Wednesday?" A grin tugged at the corners of his mouth. "Unless you come up with some other project between now and then."

CATHY'S CHRISTMAS CONFESSION

AFTER DAVID LEFT, CATHY SPENT A LONG TIME READING HER Bible and praying, asking God what He had in mind for Wednesday. *What should I do, Lord? Make a public announcement? I don't know what to do here. Please show me.*

Her thoughts turned to David. *Lord, I like him. A lot. Do you have plans for a future for us? Or aren't You ready to reveal that to me yet? Maybe he's just someone You put in my path for me to help and now he'll go on his way to someone else. Help me to accept Your will, Lord. Whatever that is.*

Cathy walked into her small office and returned her Bible to its place on her bookshelf. She stopped and stared. Of course. Christmas cards. Two boxes of unused cards. What better way to spread a message than with a personalized handwritten note in a Christmas card?

The next morning, she called Krystin.

"I have an idea that will clear my conscience and maybe increase your business."

"Clear your conscience about what?"

"Krystin, I haven't been fair to you. People think I'm baking these cookies and they love them. If I reveal where I'm getting them from, you might acquire lots more business from here. Folks are already sold on your products."

"Hm. What do you plan to do?"

"Overnight express me fifty of your business cards. I need them by Wednesday. I'm going to put them in Christmas cards and distribute them at the baking contest."

∽

DAVID ANSWERED CATHY'S CALL ON THE SECOND RING. "HI, Smart Lady. What did you come up with? I've been expecting to hear from you."

"How's your handwriting?"

David chuckled. "What have you got in mind. A public letter to the paper confessing your sin of deception?"

"Something better than that. Can you be out here Tuesday evening? I'll feed you. And bring a pen."

CHAPTER 15

"This is what I want you to print. It's all written out for you."
He picked up the piece of paper and read.

Happy Birthday Jesus.

Below that, print out:

For God so loved the world that he gave his one and only Son, that whoever believes in him shall not perish but have eternal life John 3:16 (NIV).

At the bottom of the card, write:

Do you know the Christmas story? Find it here. Luke chapter 2 verses 1-18.

He gave her an incredulous look. "And you want me to write all that on fifty cards?"

She smiled. "No. Just twenty-five. I'll do half. Don't seal the envelopes. My niece is sending me business cards. I'll need to put one in each when they arrive tomorrow."

He rubbed the back of his neck. "And we're distributing these where?"

"I've been in touch with Santa Noel. He's going to allow me to make an announcement just before the contest judging. Everyone should be there. Then we'll hand out the cards. One per family."

His eyebrows shot up. "And how are you going to manage that?"

She shrugged. "God gave me the idea. He'll help me figure it out."

"I believe He probably will. You're amazing."

"No. He is."

"By the way." He sniffed. "It smells wonderful in here. What are you feeding me?"

She pointed to a crock pot on the counter. "Pot roast, potatoes, and carrots. Still haven't mastered the oven."

He laughed. "I'm not complaining."

She narrowed her eyes and snapped her fingers. "Get busy. No food until at least ten of those cards are done."

He picked up his pen and meticulously wrote out the message. "How do we sign them?"

"I hadn't thought of that." She bit her lip. "Suggestions?"

"How about Cathy and David?"

Her face turned scarlet. "I don't know. That kind of sounds like we're a couple."

David leaned close with a grin and gazed into her eyes. "Aren't we?"

She took a sharp intake of breath. "Are we?"

"I'd like to be."

Her voice shook. "If it's okay with you, it's more than fine with me."

He put down his pen. "In that case, I have something to do first." He got up and stood next to her chair. "I am officially dating a special lady." He bent down and kissed her cheek.

Her heart galloped in her chest.

She just wished he'd found her lips.

When David answered Cathy's call Wednesday morning, he was prepared to calm her jittered nerves. Instead, her voice held all the confidence of a seasoned public speaker about to address an audience.

"David, I received the package from Krystin with the business cards. And guess what?"

"What?" He wouldn't have been surprised if she had told him her niece had sent fifty boxes of cookies.

"She sent five-dollar coupons, fifty of them, so I can put one of them in each card too. This is going to be so exciting."

"That's great. Are you nervous?"

"A little. You'll be there and I know this is what God wants me to do. I just know it."

"Okay. I'll meet you there at three-thirty." He hesitated. "Cathy, you did take the cookies out of the freezer, right?"

She giggled. "Yes. Pathetic looking as they are. They're sitting here on the table."

"A word of advice. Keep them out of Horace's way."

CATHY WALKED INTO THE COMMUNITY CENTER TO FIND A throng of people laughing and talking. Comments like "what did you bring?" and "are you going to buy anything?" were heard as she made her way to the baking table.

Millie Munford stood behind the table with a clipboard in hand. "Cathy, I've been expecting you. I see you and David Martin entered as a team."

"Yes, we did. Here's our entry."

Millie set the container down and tore off a piece of clear food wrap. "We transfer the entries to these plates to hide the identity of the entrant. Here's your number." She opened the top and inspected the cookies. Her face fell. "I thought you'd have used royal icing. Did you perhaps assist one of the children? This looks like—"

"Canned frosting. It is." Cathy put on a wide grin. "And it's an adult entry. You'll be finding out why very soon now."

"I see." Millie responded with a thin smile. "Thanks."

A lady she didn't know stepped up behind Cathy with a cake decorated with white icing, bordered by green fringe around the edges with a Christmas tree in the center.

"That looks lovely."

The lady smiled. "Thank you. This is my first attempt at cake decorating."

Cathy's eyes widened. "You may have a career in the making."

She moved on to go find David. He was engrossed in earnest conversation with a man she didn't know. He waved when she caught his attention and came to meet her.

"Did you turn the entry in?"

"Yep. We're number five in the adult judging. Millie asked if our entry was meant for the children's category."

David chuckled. "That bad, huh?"

"There are some impressive cakes over there. We probably should have opted to do a cake." She shrugged.

"Wouldn't have been near as much fun."

She punched his shoulder. "Yeah, right."

Santa Noel motioned to Cathy.

"Looks like I'll be on stage in a minute."

David grasped her hand. "I'll be up there with you."

"You don't have to do that. This is on me."

He leaned close to her ear. "I told you I'd stand beside you. I meant it."

She squeezed his hand. "Thank you."

Cathy threaded her way to the front and stood next to Santa Noel.

David hovered nearby.

Santa welcomed everyone to the contest, explained the judging rules, then turned the floor over to Cathy.

Her mouth went dry and she said a silent prayer before she spoke.

"Good afternoon, everyone. My name is Cathy Fischer. Some of you know me. I have a Christmas confession and a special Christmas message to share with you." She paused. "Many of you have enjoyed my cookie contributions to community center events, activities at Christmas Ridge Community Church, and to the food bank over the past several months. I need to confess that I have not baked those cookies. I never stated that I did, but I think many people have assumed so. I wanted to set the record straight and give credit to the person who is responsible for all those delicious cookies.

"I buy them online from Krystin Bailey's Bakery in Nashville. Krystin is my niece and that is her business. Over on the front table, you will find Christmas cards. I am asking that each family take a card and read the special message inside. You will also find a business card in each and a five-dollar coupon to be used for any product you would like to order from Krystin Bailey's Bakery in Nashville, Tennessee.

"Please accept my apology for any misunderstandings about my baking skills. To put it simply, I don't have any. I will continue to donate cookies as I have in the past, but now you also have the option to order the delicious delights of your choice.

"Enjoy the bake sale and Happy Jesus's birthday, everyone!"

The room had gone dead quiet while Cathy spoke.

When she stepped back, someone clapped. More clapping hands joined in and a voice shouted, "We love you, Cathy!"

David put his arm around her shoulders. "I'm proud of you. Do you feel better?"

A tear meandered down Cathy's cheek. "I feel great because I did what I believe God wanted me to do. Now we have to pray that people read those messages and understand the real meaning of Christmas."

A dark-haired woman wearing a walking boot approached Cathy. "Mrs. Fischer. I'm Hannah Montez, Nellie Crabtree's daughter. I wanted to thank you so much for helping my mother and for caring about her enough to check on her."

"Hannah, how nice to meet you." Cathy gestured to the boot. "I figured you had to be Nellie's daughter. How's the ankle?"

"Getting better. I still can't drive since I broke my right foot. My husband works out of town. A friend has relatives here and was able to bring me to town for a few days." She grasped Cathy's hands. "It's people like you who spread God's love. I want to thank you for that. You are a blessing."

"Thank you. How is your mom?"

Hannah released her hold and pointed with her chin. "She's over there with my neighbor. Mama has been sick on and off over the years. She's going home with me for a while, but if she gets much worse, I may have to take her back to the state hospital."

"Please keep in touch. You have my number."

"Yes, I will."

Several others approached Cathy. "We appreciated the card you sent when Jack was in the hospital." "We love you, whether you can bake or not." "We enjoyed the cookies you sent over when we had the garage roof collapse."

Marge ran up and took her by the elbow. "Cathy, I hope you don't think I valued our friendship just because of those cookies. My goodness, there is so much more to you than that. Did I give you that impression?"

"No, you never did, and perhaps I read way too much into it. I just couldn't continue to let people believe I had that kind of talent when I don't. It's a matter of honesty. I was very careful to listen. If anyone had said something about me baking the cookies, I would have set them straight right away. Did you get a Christmas card?"

"I did. Your message is lovely. I notice it's signed Cathy and David. Does that mean what I think it does?"

She smiled. "Well, it means we're willing to be recognized as a dating couple. I think we both need to get to know each other better before we move to a more serious step, but we have acknowledged our special feelings for each other."

Marge hugged her. "I'm so happy for you."

Speaking of David, where was he? She searched the room and found him standing near the stack of Christmas cards. She hurried over to him.

He met her with a grin. "You said God would help you figure out how to get these cards delivered. I guess He did. Looks like He appointed me."

She chuckled.

"If everyone would please take a seat," Santa Noel's voice boomed across the crowded room, "we will announce the winners of the First Christmas Ridge Community Center Baking Contest. We will commence the auction immediately after."

A flurry of activity ensued as people moved across the room to occupy the folding chairs set up for the occasion. Millie Munford took Santa's place and read from a piece of paper. "First, we would like to thank all of you who entered the contest. We hope you've had a chance to view these delicious looking goodies, because you will be bidding on them soon." She offered a special thank you to the judges. Rounds of clapping and cheers waxed and waned as the winners were announced, starting with the younger age categories.

Once they reached the adult category, David clasped Cathy's hand. "Nervous?"

"Not really. I'm too happy."

"First place goes to Carla Morgan, creator of this beautiful Christmas tree cake."

Cathy clutched David's sleeve. "I'm so excited for her. I saw her when we came in and she told me this is her first cake decorating attempt."

"She did a nice job."

The next two winners were cookie entries, both exquisitely decorated.

"We didn't win." David squeezed her hand.

"Did you really expect to?" She laughed. "Considering I couldn't even set the correct oven temperature, it's a wonder we even had an entry."

"Not to mention trying to add a hard-boiled egg to the mix."

Cathy overheard a lady behind them with two young children. "When we get home, Daddy and I are going to read you the story about the night Jesus was born."

Her heart warmed. She turned to David. "You said we didn't win? If we made even one person aware of the real meaning of Christmas here today, it's a win that beats any other."

CHAPTER 16

Christmas Eve morning and not a word from David. He had told her after the baking contest judging and auction he would be out of town for a few days. He had been vague about where he was going or why. She didn't feel she had the right to demand an explanation, but her heart had suffered a bruise.

He had promised he would return by Christmas Eve.

Cathy wrapped the gift she had knitted for him, a gray beanie to protect his head against the chilly winter air. She also wrapped a box of beautifully decorated Christmas cookies from Krystin's Bakery. She chose candy cane paper and decorated the gifts with small white bows. The card she had purchased said "To a Special Friend" on the front and showed a photo of two people walking along a snow-packed path into the woods with an alpine scene in the background. Inside, she printed:

DAVID
CHERISH THE PAST – EMBRACE THE FUTURE.

Below the printed verse, she wrote:

HAPPY JESUS'S BIRTHDAY.
MAY YOU FIND CHRISTMAS JOY.
BLESSINGS
CATHY.

Should she have signed it love?

She placed the gifts under the tree with those she had received from Krystin, Marge, and Pastor Hewitt.

She set out for the church. The sanctuary exuded peace on the eve of the Savior's arrival into the world. The nativity scene beckoned to her. She knelt at the front railing. Cathy thought about the first Christmas, trying to picture the baby Jesus in a lowly manger. She imagined herself in Mary's place, a young girl in her teens, unmarried and with child, trying to understand what was happening to her.

Cathy had carried a child twice for a short time, but she had never borne a baby. She could not relate to the experience of childbirth. What would it have been like for that young woman to travel so far on a donkey, no less, only to learn there was no soft bed to lie on after her journey? To give birth in a smelly stable with the noise and stench of animals must have been horrific. Yet, Mary had endured childbirth with joy, knowing God had given her such a special task. Mother to the Savior of the world. What a unique and amazing way God had manifested His love for His children.

She prayed a prayer of thanksgiving for all God had done

CATHY'S CHRISTMAS CONFESSION

for her this past year and asked for His blessings for the future. She prayed for David's safe return. What plans did their Heavenly Father have in store for them?

She retrieved the bulletins from the office and set them on the back table. She had printed twice as many as she usually did for regular Sunday mornings. Non-churchgoers tended to be drawn to the Christmas Eve service.

The small candles with their drip protectors lay in a basket. She took a quick count to be sure there were at least a hundred.

When she left the church, Cathy couldn't resist a drive past the Pine Street apartments. No sign of David's vehicle in the lot. Perhaps bad weather had delayed him. *Please, Lord, keep him safe.*

A single car was parked in front of the funeral home. How sad that any family should have to grieve their loved one on Christmas Eve. Her gaze snapped to the name printed on the sign in front of the building. MAYBELLE LOVEJOY.

Was her son inside? She had to stop.

She opened the door and trod lightly down the center aisle of the small chapel. A man and woman stood around the casket in front with a young girl between them. They all looked her way as she approached.

"Hi. I'm sorry if this is family time and I'm intruding. My name is Cathy Fischer."

All three greeted her with a warm smile.

"You must be John and Missy." Cathy extended her hand to the man. "I met your mom for only a few moments, but she touched me in a very special way. I'm so sorry for your loss."

John gave her a warm handshake. "Don't be sad for us, Mrs. Fischer. Mom is right where she wanted to be this

143

Christmas. She told us she'd be celebrating in style this year. She is."

Tears came to Cathy's eyes. "She told me the very same thing the day I met her. She gave me a message to share Christmas joy."

Missy stepped forward. "You did."

"What?" Cathy looked at her in bewilderment.

"We have one of your Christmas cards. This is our granddaughter, Mandy. She entered the baking contest at the community center."

Cathy's hands flew to her mouth. "Oh, my."

"When we showed the card to Mom, her face lit up with pure delight. She said God had led her to the right person to share Christmas joy. She saw your name on the card and knew it had to be you."

Tears poured down Cathy's cheeks. "It's amazing how God arranges little encounters in our lives. Happy Jesus's birthday to you all."

CATHY HOVERED BY THE FRONT DOOR AND PRAYED FOR DAVID to come sauntering up the walk. She pasted on a smile and waited in vain as a steady stream of worshipers entered the sanctuary. Her stomach flipped. Where was he? Why hadn't he called?

Her heart lightened when Donna and Dennis Walker greeted her. She went inside and sat with them. Cathy succumbed to tears when voices came together in harmony as *Joy to the World* filled the sanctuary. Tears of joy and sadness both as she reflected on this emotional day and what lay ahead.

Joy over the Savior's presence.

Sadness over David's absence.

Her emotions vacillated between disappointment and fear. David had promised he would be here for Christmas Eve.

Could she trust his promises?

What if something happened to him?

As the service drew to its conclusion, the soft strains of *Silent Night* drifted from the organ. Marge played the hymn with a light touch of her fingers that communicated the tranquility of this wondrous night.

The lights went out.

One by one, the candles pierced the darkness.

Ushers moved silently to light the candles of those who sat on the aisle, then parishioners lit each other's on down the pews.

Cathy held her candle steady, careful not to tip it and drip wax on the pew or the floor.

"That was very moving." Dennis guided the women toward the back of the church.

"We've been reading your Bible," Donna added. "We talked about coming to church. We're glad we came tonight."

"It's a joy to see you here. We'd love to have you come back." Cathy clasped hands with her friends. "Happy Jesus's birthday."

DAVID WAITED IN THE BACK OF THE SANCTUARY AND exchanged Christmas greetings as worshipers exited the church. He searched for Cathy and put on a big smile when he saw her walking toward him with Donna and Dennis Walker.

Her lips formed a ruled line when she spotted him. Tear stains blotted her cheeks.

His heart lurched. How disappointed she must have been.

"David. Where were you?"

Her tone carried a sharp edge. Was she angry or worried?

"I am so sorry." He put his arm around her shoulders. "I got caught in a snowstorm on the interstate. Traffic moved at a crawl, accidents everywhere."

She relaxed against him and sighed with relief. "Thank God you're safe."

"I wanted to be here for this service. I hated to miss it." He leaned close. "And being with you."

She smiled. "It was a beautiful service." She hesitated a moment. "Where did you go?"

He squeezed her closer. "We need to talk."

She shot him an inquisitive glance. "Sounds serious."

"It is."

A light snow was falling when they stepped outside. "Just enough snow for a fresh dusting to wake up to on Christmas morning." Cathy pulled on her gloves.

He brushed snow from his sleeve. "A winter wonderland."

"I have a gift for you at my house. Would you like to come out this evening and open it or wait until tomorrow?"

He grinned. "Let me guess. A box of cookies."

"Aw, you spoiled all the fun." She pouted. "There is a little something else under my tree for you."

"I have a special gift for you, too, and I need to give it to you at your house. There's a reason."

Her eyes shone with anticipation. "You certainly have me curious."

He winked. "I'll see you there in a few minutes."

CATHY'S CHRISTMAS CONFESSION

When David stepped inside Cathy's house, the Christmas tree was lit and Christmas music played softly from the stereo. A warm fire crackled in the fireplace. He grasped Horace's paw in a handshake. "Merry Christmas, Horace." The dog ambled to his favorite spot in front of the fireplace and flopped down on the rug.

David chuckled and kissed Cathy's cheek.

"Let me get us some coffee to go with the cookies you know I'm giving you." She took his jacket and handed him the wrapped gift.

"You could have pretended I guessed wrong." He waited until she returned with the coffee before he opened the package. His mouth watered when he saw the colorful treats.

"That's what real baked Christmas cookies are supposed to look like." She grinned and handed him his second gift with the card on top.

"I guess ours were pretty pathetic." He laughed and opened the card. "What a beautiful message." His eyes widened as he pulled the knitted hat from its box. "You made this, didn't you?"

She nodded. "I know you have a full head of hair, but I worry about you catching cold."

"Thank you." He kissed her forehead. "That's so thoughtful."

"I wanted to give you something that would remind you of this Christmas season and all the time we've spent together."

"Oh, I'll remember." His expression turned serious. "I have to tell you where I was for two days and why." He cleared his throat. "I went to see Heather."

Cathy blinked.

"She was laid to rest in Fairmount Cemetery in Denver. I

had to say a final good-bye and tell her it's time for me to move on. And it is time. Now I want to give you your gift, but you have to open it in your kitchen."

She shot him a bewildered look. "That's an odd request."

David gave her a teasing smile. They sat at the table with their coffee mugs in front of them. "I wanted to come out here on this special night because this is a special place and I have something special to tell you in it."

She looked around and back to him. "My house? Or my kitchen?"

"Both." He reached into his pocket. His hands shook when he pulled out the small box wrapped in green Christmas paper with a white bow. "I don't want to rush you into anything—" he pressed the gift into her hand—" but I want you to know how I feel about you."

Her fingers trembled and her cheeks flamed as she removed the bow and laid it on the table.

David pointed toward the bow with a nod of his chin. "Pastor Hewitt told me white symbolizes joy. Did you know that?"

"No, I didn't." She unwrapped the box and peered inside. A tiny diamond winked from a ring of white gold. She gasped. "David, it's lovely."

"Not as lovely as you. I wanted to give it to you here. Right at this table where you shared your Christmas confession. It's where I found Christmas joy. I love the sincerity in your soul and the warmth in your heart." He took the ring and slipped it onto her finger. "I love you."

"Oh, David." Tears shimmered in her eyes. "I love you too."

"I had to visit Heather because I couldn't do this until I

had." He stood, pulled her into his arms, and covered her soft lips with his. "I'll always cherish the past, but I'm ready to embrace the future. When you marry me, if you marry me, there will always be three of us."

Her face clouded.

"You, me, and God. I won't turn my back on Him again."

She wrapped her arms around his neck and pulled him close.

"Happy Jesus's birthday, my love."

ACKNOWLEDGMENTS

Many thanks to RL Ashly and F. Tilly Browne for inviting me to be a part of the Christmas Ridge Romance series. Thank you to the two of you along with Donna Schlachter and Daneen Padilla for the encouragement and brainstorming along the way.

Thank you to my critique group, Scribes 236 through American Christman Fiction Writers, for all of the wisdom, suggestions, and advice you have shared with me over these past few years. Even though you did not get to critique all of this project, I heard each of your voies as I typed words on the page.

Thank you to my editor Kathy KcKinsey and beta readers David Parks and Becky Van Vleet. You offered helpful suggestions and corrected my errors.

Thank you to Marlene Bagnull and her Thursday morning and evening critique groups. Your support and encouragement were most appreciated.

Thank you to Gwen and Jerry for all the Scrabble game photos you texted to me.

Thank you to Janice Hanna Thompson for the baking advice! If you really want to learn about baking, check out her amazing website. www.Outoftheboxbaking.com.

Thank you to my church family at First Presbyterian

Church Las Animas for praying me through this writing project.

Thank you to family and friends who supported me with your thoughts, prayers, and words of encouragement.

First and foremost, thank you, Lord, for the gift of your Son, Jesus, the Creator of Christmas Joy.

ABOUT THE AUTHOR

Patti Shene Gonzales hosts *Step Into the Light*, a weekly interview style podcast, where guests share their journey out of darkness or ways they lead others out of darkness.

She hosts writers on her two blogs, *Patti's Porch* and *The Over 50 Writer*.

Patti enjoyed a thirty-year career as a psychiatric nurse and has always harbored a desire to write. *Cathy's Christmas Confession* released in November 2022 and is her first full-length published work.

Patti enjoys writing, reading, critiquing, and spending time with family and friends. She lives in Colorado with her devoted feline companion, Duncan.

Connect with Patti at: www.pattishene.com

facebook.com/pattishene
twitter.com/pattishene

Made in the USA
Middletown, DE
11 June 2023